VISIONS OF PLEASURE

ENGLISH ROSE SERIES 1

CLAIR BRETT

COPYRIGHT

DEDICATION

I am dedicating this book to anybody who doesn't know their own worth. We are all fallible and quirky, and eccentric. Believe in your gifts and skills. Understand that we are all just faking it till we make it. Embrace you! Once you do that, you will attract the people who will embrace you too. Remember the worst critics and haters speak to their own fears and shortcomings when they speak about others.

Northwest Spain, 1813

My Dear Senor Guaire,

I have just finished reading your most recent reply to my letter and I have to say that I am very disappointed. The situation has gotten quite horrible. My sister Constance was stopped and openly questioned about the rumors of my family's deadly deeds. She did not know how to respond, and so had to just walk away from the awful, dreadful scene. I fear that if this goes on much longer, there will not need to be any actual evidence or proof of wrong doing, for our family name will be ruined for good. My father has taken to his library and will not allow any discussion of the allegations whatsoever. I am at my wits end. I respect your predicament and your responsibilities to your family and lands, but I do not know who else to turn to. This will mean ruin for myself and my sisters, it may well be too late for myself, but Constance and Maria should not have to suffer if I can do anything about it.

I beg of you to take pity on us and come post haste to aid us in proving my ancestors are not murderers or land thieves.

Sincerely yours,
The Honorable Aisling Lightowler

CHAPTER 1

*B*astion threw the note atop a pile of papers strewn across the desk. Miguel his butler had been told no more letters from Miss Lightowler, and yet here one lies. "Miguel!"

A man didn't have to have visions to hear the desperation in the words, or to understand the import of her plea. Thanks to his gift however, Miss Lightowler sitting at a writing desk, penning each word with tears streaming down soft pink cheeks a clear image. No sobbing, or hiccupping for this one, no bigger than a sprite, if his vision held true, but she was tough.

Bastion ran his finger down the parchment as it laid staring up at him, feeling the raised bumps and twirls of the ink. His gut clenched, and in a second yanked into a vision. This one, however not of the beautiful English girl.

The vision swelled in waves around him, it tossed him like a toy boat in a bath hitting the floor retching with the motion and pain wracking his body.

A house with people grouped around came into view. A large crowd impeded a full view of the house. Bastion clenched his eyes shut, giving into the vision more. *The scent of fire from the torches the people held filled the room, then something—fear so palpable you could smell it sharp and acidic, like the smell of strong coffee in his cup when brought to his lips. Someone in that house was scared, and not just one someone, many. The fear coursed through him, owned him, panic rising to his chest. these people were his, but how?*

With a jerk, the vision shifted to a familiar one. *Miss Lightowler stood facing him smiling, her long hair flowed around her like a cloud. She reached up and cupped his cheek with a tiny hand. White hot desire shot through his body.* Oh, Lord, this spelled trouble. Never had a reaction to a woman come with such force, and they hadn't even met. But from the first letter, the visions intensified becoming more explicit with each one. By traveling to England Bastion would be securing his bedding of Miss Lightowler. It was a truth deep set. A vision always ran the course.

"Miguel! Damn it, where are you?" Bastion bellowed managing to get onto his feet and stagger to the drink trolley and took several linen clothes to clean up the floor.

"Yes, Count?" Miguel strolled into the room and stopped seeing Bastion on the floor cleaning up after himself. "I can—"

"No need, it is done, and I am rather tired of having to remind you I do not want to be called count. The count was my brother, who chose to go and get himself killed."

"Yes, senor," Miguel amended.

"I thought I told you I wanted no more letters from Miss Lightowler forwarded to me."

"Yes Senor, you did."

"Why is it, when I am searching for the land papers from the solicitors do I find a salver of letters with that on top sitting on the desk?" Bastion asked pointing to the open letter splayed out.

"Because I put it there Senor."

"You defied my wishes?"

"Yes, Senor," Miguel answered no remorse shown in those intelligent eyes.

Bastion glared. His brother thought him a paragon and his nephew adored him as well. Niall had already lost so much when Louis got himself killed, Bastion would not take away another person in Niall's life, not to mention Bastion was certain Miguel had been on staff for as long as the family owned the property.

"Where are the damned papers from the solicitor?" choosing to change the subject. The letter could be thrown out.

"I assumed you were finished with them yesterday when you signed them, so I put them away until the solicitor could pick them up." Miguel answered and

"No, I just felt I should check them again, but if you say they are ready to go, I will take your word."

" I will set them over here at your table, so you can look at them at your leisure." The graying Spaniard plodded over and set them on the table knowing Bastion refused to acknowledge the desk of the Count. "When you are finished that, Coun–Senor Bastion, I would think there is nothing more for you today. I need to take some time to, ah, organize things. There is nothing pressing to be finished at this time."

Bastion barked with bitter laughter, "there is always something pressing to be done Miguel. Always."

Miguel's subtle wince caught Bastion's eye, "Yes, I suppose it would seem so."

Bastion grunted his reply.

"Your latest periodicals have arrived. Perhaps you can take the time to read through some of them." Miguel offered.

Bastion saw it for the peace offering and distraction it was but didn't care. Thinking back to a time not so many months ago more suited to the correct workings of the house; Louis would have handled the day to day of the lands and people, while Bastion poured over the archaeological journals and periodicals. They were a bible and a balm that soothed him as the past did. The present, or more specifically his present did anything but. Filled with cannon fodder, political suicide and murder.

Worst yet, the visions were neither timely nor optimistic. Bones were safe, however. Receiving visions from bones never hurt anyone, because their stories had already played out.

"Thank you. I think I will."

"Oh, and I will put Miss Lightowler's letter with them." Miguel added.

"No. I am not going to England."

"That girl is in trouble, and it appears the part of you that has been your lifelong burden could in fact help her. Not to mention it would get you away from here for a bit."

"With the upheaval and the eventual return of King Ferdinand, oh, and my nephew, don't you think I should be here in Spain and try to bring these lands back into the fold of the conservatives?"

"With these papers, that is done." Miguel pointed to the papers on the table, ready to go to the solicitors, "and I am certain you have no interest in being here for Ferdinand's homecoming. I know how you feel about the politics of late, so you may not use that as an excuse. The farms will continue to work without you on the property, and Niall can be cared for by a nurse and a tutor."

"I will not abandon my nephew, my only known relative, to run off to England and dig around in the dirt. The boy has known nothing but abandonment his whole life. First his mother abandons him to a father too caught up in politics to notice, now Louis is killed. The poor boy was thrown in with a group of adults who thought of their own desires and not well-being of a child. That stops with me," Bastion ground out.

Bastion hated saying anything bad about his deceased brother, but he argued repeatedly with Louis to be careful of too strong political affiliations in the turmoil that was the Spanish government with Ferdinand's exile; begged him to think about Niall.

"Perhaps you could take him with you," Miguel raised a hand to silence Bastion, who stood arms crossed, feet spread, holding himself silent, but only just. "It has been a horrible ordeal, and a change of scenery would do the boy well. You could bring along a nurse and tutor, so it would not be a distraction to your work."

Miguel had a good point. The boy could use a change. The five-year-old spent any free time curled up in his father's chair by the fire, wrapped in the throw Louis used. Moving on was needed, but how to do it while surrounded by memories?

Bastion eyed the personal secretary, grunted, then walked over to the pile of periodicals with the letter lying like a viper on the top. Pausing for only a moment to glare at the letter and wish it away. When it did not vanish, he scooped up the bundle and strode out of the study without a word to Miguel, but the smile on the older man's face did nothing to improve Bastion's mood.

Once settled in his private parlor, with a pot of strong coffee and a plate of cheese and bread Bastion slid the first periodical, The British Museum's periodical of antiquities, to the top of the pile, grabbed a hunk of bread and turned to the first sheet. A favorite column that published one of William Cunnington's letters from his days of excavation in each issue started his reading. Bastion thought often what it would have been like to sit with the man and ask him more questions than could be counted. It was a true loss to the world when Cunnington passed away in 1810.

The posted letter this month once again had been to one of the many wealthy patrons. The amount of detail always amazed. Bastion unwound the string on a tattered notebook on the table gingerly and opened the leather binding to a blank page close to the back and with charcoal in hand began taking notes.

The visions gave him much more information and clues than men like Cunnington would have ever been afforded, but to be taken seriously there had to be subterfuge and strict adherence to professional mannerisms and conduct. A good thirty minutes passed before it started. A quick sharp zing to the temple with white spots coming to his sight. Damn. Bastion hoped to avoid the note long enough to calm any frayed senses from the frustrations of the morning. It was easier to control the intensity of the visions with a calm mind. Not to mention the ill effects from the impact of the earlier ones still haunted him. The periodical dropped to his lap and a hand flew to the side of his head to try and stop the sharp pains. As soon as the vision had its way, the pain would stop.

Sighing heavily with resignation, Bastion picked up the letter, leaving the news sheet forgotten. The letter buzzed in Bastion's hand. A warmth seeped from the velum into his palm, as if the last person to touch it held it long enough to make it warm. The addresses were written in a light, airy script now quite familiar on sight. She had beautiful handwriting, Bastion thought. Letter released the familiar bright smell of jasmine and oranges. it wafted out of the pages of the letter to intoxicate. How many letters crossed three countries from this woman asking for him to come? Five? Maybe six, but everyone with the same effect.

Reopening the letter made the pages vibrate harder, one could almost see them shivering in the sunlight that spread across the room in the early afternoon light. The letter landed back on top of the pile. No need to read the words again.

Bastion knew what had to happen next. Not just to help her, but to get answers for him and Niall about their past, because the people gripped in fear in the first vision were not the Lightowlers.

"Damn!" he swore to the empty room rising to go fetch Miguel and have the travel plans made, and to instruct Niall's nurse that the boy would be going on a trip and would need to have a trunk packed. They were going to England, and Bastion would be coming home with answers, and Lord only knew what else, but for once in his life, Bastion Niall Dalais Guaire, 4th Count of Lugar de Sueno refused to be driven by a vision. There would be no marriage to the strong-willed wisp of a woman with long dark hair and big, overly bright eyes. He had no need or use for a wife and an English one to boot.

"Damn," He said again, for good measure.

CHAPTER 2

"What the devil has you in such a state?" asked
Maria, Aisling Lightowler's youngest and quite
honestly most difficult sister, according to Aisling.

"Nothing, just the post arrived without a response from The
Count of Lugar de Sueno." Aisling admitted. She had given her
own letter a month ago to get to its destination, now searching
the post every morning when it might arrive. Nothing.

Aisling turned her back on the table where the morning
post sat with letters for her father and sisters. There was only
one letter of interest and it hadn't been delivered. Having never
done the social rounds outside the community the only friends
were no more than a morning's walk away no need for mailed
correspondence and that fit perfectly into her idea of life, but
since the rumors began few people reached out any longer
Aisling padded to the settee and took up her mending. To be
embroidering some beautiful skirt edge, or even a blanket
would be lovely, but mending came first. Once through the pile
of shirts father had all but destroyed in the rose garden, she

might be able to get back to the lovely design that had taken weeks to make progress on, on best evening dress. She sighed heavily.

"Well, as far as I can see it is a blessing. You have never gotten a positive response from the man, and I think you should give up." Maria advised, glancing through the newssheet she borrowed from the housekeeper who probably nicked it from Lord Glendale's daughter after giving it to her staff once finished with it. No doubt it was at least three or more months hold.

"We need to do something, Maria. We cannot just sit back and let this horrible story grow bigger by the second." Aisling tried to reason.

"Posh. It will all just die away. Once I have gone to London and married well, no one will dare speak ill of papa."

"I am dearly heartened by your plan, except for a few flaws." Aisling said with exasperation, sick of this conversation, "You are the youngest, and should not be going out to have a season until the rest of us are settled," putting up a hand to keep her sister quiet until she was finished. "How do you suggest that the three of us find said husbands to open the world to you, when not one upstanding neighbor will publicly invite or include us in any social event? Not to mention that two of the suitors Deidra was giving account to, up and stopped visiting and writing not more than a fort night ago. We are going to be truly lost if something doesn't happen."

Maria looked at Aisling with a slight glimmer of tears in her eyes. Aisling knew Maria was not so cotton headed to not understand the potential for ruin in this situation. She understood much better than father, but ever the optimist, Maria chose to think it would blow over.

Aisling knew better, "I feel strongly that I will get the answer

I am seeking with this letter." "Are you expecting guests?" Constance, Aisling's middle sister stepped into the room, still wearing the clay covered apron and sculpting smock used to cover her dress while she worked.

"No. No one, why?" Aisling asked.

"Because a large traveling carriage and another smaller servant's carriage just rolled up. Perhaps they think they are at Lord Glendale's." Constance answered.

The three women went to the window in the parlor looking onto the drive and to Aisling's surprise, the carriages were not making the slow turn to leave. The driver had dismounted from the larger carriage instructing the other one to do the same.

Before stairs could be posted at the door to the main vehicle the door opened, and the largest man Aisling had ever seen emerged. The narrow opening of the door swelled releasing his massive shoulders. Once out with turned his back to the house, she was afforded a view of where those shoulders went. His jacket stretched across his back and seemed to be hugging his upper arms. From his shoulders Aisling could see his figure with the cut of his clothing, which tapered down to a trim waist, which gave way to what looked like soft as skin breeches that were just a snug as the jacket. Oh my! Aisling stepped back from the window feeling too hot for her own comfort. Whoever this was, they had never been introduced. She would have remembered him.

"Oh, who's the little boy?" Constance asked out loud. "He is darling!"

Aisling took a calming breath and returned to the window in time to see the larger than life man, lifting a young boy no bigger than five years old from the carriage and propping him on his hip in a familiar way. The boy said something, then placed on the ground to run over to an older man exiting the smaller carriage. The behemoth turned fully toward the house.

Oh, my Lord. Aisling could not breathe. His hair was as black as night and shown in the sunlight. The sun glinted off the wave or curl longer than what she thought the current style as his hat couldn't begin to cover the length and held back with a tie at his nape. His skin too sun kissed, and much darker than the pale young men in this area. The gardeners or farmers who spent their days in the sun working more resembled this man. Whoever this was, and once they directed him to his true destination, she would not soon forget him.

He turned and walked out of sight of the window, and within moments the bell peeled at the door. Aisling moved away from the window and toward the hallway to answer the door. While they could afford a cook and part time housekeeper, and butler a large staff of doorman stretched well beyond their funds. Aisling stood looking at the unopened door hoping to find steady footing. She had never spoken to a man so beautiful, and dearly hoped her tongue would not become tied. The bell peeled a second time.

"Answer it." prodded Maria. Aisling shushed her waving a hand and reached for the knob.

The old door creaked open to its entirety. "Yes, may I help you?" Aisling asked, trying not to choke on her words faced with such an Adonis, towering in the open doorway. She was wrong, his jacket wasn't hugging him, but holding on for purchase, lifting his arm to remove his hat and bow, she swore it might rip open at the strain.

"Yes, I am looking for The Honorable Aisling Lightowler, or perhaps Viscount Lightowler if she is not available."

Aisling stared, blinked, then stared some more. What would this person want from her? The heavy accent of Spanish with a bit of French gave him away as a traveler. "I am she, but I fear I am at a loss, for I don't believe I am familiar with you." Aisling managed a bit bolstered by her confidence.

"Miss Lightowler, we have not met or been introduced in person, no. I am Bastion Guaire. We have been conversing back and forth for months."

The gentleman stopped and stood silent looking at her for a response. He had come. She had told her sisters it would happen, but in all honesty didn't truly believe it herself.

"Oh, Oh, yes, Count Sueno–"

"Please, Bastion or Mr. Guaire if you must. I am still too new to the title, I am not comfortable with it."

"Ah," Aisling searched her brain for the appropriate reply. There had to be–

"Mr. Guaire, please come in. If you must just step around Aisling." She heard Constance speaking, and had enough wits to step out of the way. Bastion Guaire the archeologist from the journals and essays stood in the doorway, happened to be the only thought rattling in her head. She squared her shoulders, took a deep breath and pushed past the utter loss of any clear thought. "Mr. Guaire, I expected a letter. We would have had things prepared for you and your guests–"

"I considered sending a letter ahead, but with travel the way it is right now, with the war I was not certain another ship would be available any time in the near future, so instead, I took the ship that would have brought my letter. I could pen one to you now if that would help."

She smiled despite herself at his jest. "No, not at all. We are familiar with the unrest on the peninsula and understand. We are thankful you chose to come so soon. Maria, please go find Deidra and ask Mrs. Hascomb to ready the guest suite. How many rooms will you require Mr. Guaire?" Aisling asked turning toward her new guest. His eyes were a soft brown, the color of warm honey. She had to clear her throat.

"Two if possible. I have my nephew with me, I am his guardian, since his father died, and I could not leave him. His tutor can share his room. If that is too much trouble, we can all room together."

"No, not at all. It may take our housekeeper a bit longer to ready two rooms, is all."

"That is fine and to be expected. Is there a place my nephew can explore? He has been in the carriage too long for a young boy."

"Oh, yes, he can wander the grounds at his choice–" Aisling tried to answer, but Maria cleared her throat with a concerned look on her face.

"Oh, the rose garden, except the rose garden. Please have his tutor keep him free of that area. It is my father's vocation to study and propagate new rose species." Aisling explained.

"Of course, let me go and inform senor Perez before they wander in there." Mr. Guaire said and was back out the door in a heartbeat, or five if keeping track by the one attempting to pound out of her chest, Aisling thought. As soon as his shadow left the doorway, she could breathe again.

"My Lord, Aisling he is massive! You never told us he was such a large man." Maria gasped quietly

"I didn't know. It is not as if they have drawings of what they look like next to their essays."

"Well still. A man so large is very disconcerting. Too tall and broad if you ask me." Maria commented dryly. It definitely disconcerted Aisling but not in the way Maria meant. Aisling had envisioned a much smaller less commanding individual, more like her father. Quiet, a bit disheveled, and not all muscled and strong as this gentleman.

Marshalling her nerves Aisling calmed herself and schooled any frayed emotions as her mother taught. She wished her mother remained home. Mama would know what to say to Count Sueno, but Mama chose to visit their aunt, and had been since the ugliness had forced them to stop their daily and weekly visits in the community. She had pleaded with father to at the very least make a statement, but alas, Papa sees nothing to the rumors and does not understand why we would give credence to any of it. Mother perplexed him upon leaving, but not enough to make any promises. Papa just kissed his wife's cheek and told her to have a lovely visit.

She had wanted the girls to go as well. Aisling thought Maria would jump at the chance to be that much closer to London, but Aisling realized that all the girls, feared for their father's safety. At least with the girls in the house, they assured one another no one would try to harm them to get to their father, well hoped was a better word Aisling thought as she waited for the doorway to be filled again with a dark figure. And sure, enough within moments a large male form filled her view. Just as Constance and their other sister Deidra emerged from the hallway leading below stairs.

"Mrs. Hascomb said it would take an hour or more without help to ready two rooms. I told her that was fine and asked cook to prepare a tray with meat, cheese, and bread with tea." Constance said to Aisling but continuing to look at their guest. Aisling wasn't sure if Constance wanted to run from him or sculpt him. She would bet on the latter.

"Mr. Guaire, I would like to introduce you to my other sister, Deidra." Aisling motioned toward her next oldest sister who stood with a similar look to Constance. At least she wasn't the only one affected.

"Miss Lightowler, it is a pleasure." Bastion took her hand

and bowed. For such a large man, his manners and easy grace spoke of a person comfortable with himself and his station.

"Why don't we go into the parlor and await the respite. I am sure you are hungry."

"Yes, to tell the truth, we have been traveling for upwards of a week after we landed, and while the food at traveling inns is more than acceptable, there just doesn't seem to be enough." Aisling bit back a giggle, At the Count's obvious angst about the amount of food offered in English establishments. Perhaps cook should be warned to plate more food. The whole ensemble made their way into the parlor.

Marie hurried to collect the forgotten sewing just left when they first greeted their guest.

"Please, have a seat." Aisling wondered what had happened to her sisters. They all seemed to have lost their voices collectively. "Again, I am so glad you decided to come. I became fearful that your last letter would be the last of the correspondence. I am not sure what we would have done."

The count settled in a chair leaving the couch for the sisters, but Aisling feared for the sturdiness of the chair in question. They did not live in squalor, but roses did not pay such a handsome income. Their belongings had been handed down over many generations and maintained well, but she feared they were not prepared for a French, Spanish count.

"Yes, well I will be honest with you, I am not certain I will be able to do anything to assist you, but I am willing to try." His discomfort plain to see. Just as Aisling was going to ask if he quite well, Pilchard came bustling in with a tray. Her visitor's eyes lit up and seemed to clear like they had been hazed over.

"Ah, this looks scrumptious! Far better than the meager offerings at the posting inns. You may have just saved me from starvation."

Pilchard beamed, "I will make sure to pass that along to the cook." For the duration of his stay, cook would save the best cuts and largest portions for him now. Once the plates were set, the butler left the group alone again.

"Is it as tasty as it is generous?" Constance asked the Count.

"Oh, yes. I must admit, I was despairing at my choice to come to England after the third night or so, when we were fed yet another rabbit stew, with no seasoning, and very meager vegetables. Not at all like the heavily spiced meals I am given at home, but this cold venison is very flavorful, and well-seasoned. And the bread is obviously fresh this morning."

Aisling watched the family's would be savior take a large bite and close his eyes, sighing. A strange shock wave tore through Aisling's body. Her calm smile slipped, and chills raised the hair on her arms. What happened to her she didn't know, but his eyes locked with hers filled with a recognition that unsettled Aisling deeply.

"Well, Count Sueno," Aisling pushed forward to get beyond whatever moment they just shared.

"Please call me Bastion or Mr. Guaire. As I said before, I am new to the title and am not comfortable with it. We are not in society, so I see no reason for such rules."

"Very well, Mr. Guaire, how would you like to get started? I assume you would like a day or so to rest after such a journey."

"Oh, no. Not at all. I am eager to get started. As soon as we entered the property, I became connected to the history here. I will need to be brought up to date on the history of your issue. Perhaps later this afternoon you can accompany me to the grave you mentioned." "That would be fine. I am sure Mari–"

Her sister gave a quick head jerk to indicate she would not be going anywhere.

"I am sure Deidra would be happy–"

"Sorry, I promised father I would help him this afternoon, he is working on grafting two specimens and it requires more than two hands."

"Ok, well, Constance, would you be available this afternoon, to go with us to the grave?" She waited for Constance to acknowledge, but she appeared too busy scribbling on a sheet of paper to notice. Deidra nudged Constance and she looked up unaware of the attention.

"What? Oh, I am sorry."

"Will you be available to go with Mr. Guaire and myself to the grave this afternoon?"

"I suppose so, yes." Aisling answered, but knew that look. As soon as Constance got back into her sculpting studio all would be forgotten. Constance would have to be collected before meeting up with their guest.

Mrs. Hascomb entered and informed them that the larger of the two rooms was complete and ready for the Count, but she would need assistance moving another bed into the other room, as it only held one at the moment. Deidra excused herself to be of assistance, and after rising when Deidra left, Senor Guaire also left to go to his room and get settled, but without a large hunk of bread and the rest of the venison tucked inside.

Aisling released the breath she had been holding since the Fourth Count of Lugar de Sueno sauntered into her home.

"Oh, my Lord, Aisling. Whatever are you going to do with him? I hardly think he will go unnoticed. I thought you wanted to keep our research quiet as to not arise suspicion."

"That had been my hope, but I am afraid you are correct Maria, this gentleman will never be able to go about the countryside and not be noticed. I am afraid we will just have to weather the storm."

CHAPTER 3

*B*astion closed the door to his small, yet neatly appointed room and breathed a sigh of relief. His whole body had begun to hum as they made the trip up the drive even before laying eyes on the woman. Once faced with the very woman who had been plaguing his waking visions and sleeping dreams for almost five months, devouring Miss Lightowler in the entry hall had been an option.

The sisters were all very different in their looks and demeanors. The youngest one, Marie he thought, walking to the trunk that had found its way to his room. Bastion hoped they had at least one sturdy young man on staff to lift such heavy objects, reaching in and pulling out a clean shirt, before his thoughts went back to the little slip of a girl that was the younger sister. Hair, a mop of curls barely confined in the coiffure atop her head. She would have been the picture of an English lady. Blond with blue eyes and pale skin. Not at all like the Spanish women.

Deidra, the older sister, Bastion considered her while

pulling off his shirt and ambling to the water basin to clean the road dust from his person. That sister would not be counted a fool, and as the oldest, seemed in charge of the house. Where was the mother? dead? As far as Bastion could tell, the Viscount could also be nonexistent, as it appeared no one bothered to gain his attention for any reason.

The middle sister reminded Bastion of himself. She appeared to be some sort of an artist. Dry and calloused hands greeted him, and she wore a very serviceable dress, meant for working not entertaining. He smiled thinking about Aisling's deep sigh at catching her sister completely in another world doodling on a scrap of paper.

Bastion got a pang of nostalgia thinking about how his brother used to do the same thing, when Bastion would be occupied with some essay, or book. If his vision played out, as they always did, would Aisling spend the rest of her life perplexed and exasperated by him, or take it in stride as she appeared to do with Constance.

Both older sisters like their younger counterparts, were a part of the fashionable attire, very much English beauties. Bastion found it rather surprising they were all finding it so difficult to secure husbands.

Then there was Aisling. Nothing like any of the others. By far the smallest of the four, standing perhaps midway up his upper arm, a wisp of a thing. Her dark tresses which appeared as long as she was tall, were pinned at the top of her head, with several unruly tendrils laying around an angelic face and trailing down a straight, proud back. Impossibly large eyes giving her the look of a fairy. The effect of gray-green eyes framed by dark hair and lashes made them a predominant feature.

The new shirt smelled of clean linen not rode dirt and

sweat. Smiling at the memory of Aisling trying to school her features into a bored smile. It might have worked expect for the eyes. They gave away her attraction. The response to his reaction to the flavorful food proved it. The little English miss would spend the day discomfited, as she desperately tried to find an ally to go with her.

Along with a tiny figure everything about this woman was petite. Perhaps a fairy come to life, just playing at being a girl. Even her ears had a slight curve at the top that one could mistake for a point. Or was it elves that had pointed ears? He didn't care. The effect just added to the allure.

He dried his face and rummaged through his toiletries for a bag with his shaving things. He didn't need to shave again today, but, would put some aftershave on to help keep the smell as likeable as he could. A full bath would be a top priority, but for now the sandalwood oil would have to do.

Once cleaned up and dressed, Bastion also grabbed his tools setting in the top of the trunk lid, strapped in by a length of ribbon. He knew where they were headed, but she was wholly unaware and as a proper lady would not come easily to his bed until persuaded. For the moment Bastion would concentrate on the problem at hand, letting Aisling come round naturally.

Giving himself a cursory glance in the window while grabbing his tools, notebook, and pencil to make sure he was more presentable than his travel self. notes would be imperative on his findings and feelings when he entered the grave site and unearthed the bones where they lay.

Bastion left his room, with a new vigor. Yes, the clean shirt and sandalwood smell helped, but his body hummed with energy he hadn't experienced in months. This outing nothing more than an excuse to spend time with his new little fairy queen.

At the top of the stairs voices trailed up from the ground floor, one of them Aisling.

"You must go with us, Constance, you must. I cannot be caught alone with the Count. You know that."

"But, I have a fabulous idea for a sculpture. It will be just fine." Constance went on, in less hushed tones than Aisling. It annoyed Bastion to think about having a chaperone, but she was wise to be concerned, more so than anyone else. "I don't care. You are coming, it is settled. Bring along a notepad if you must to make your notes and drawings, but you are coming." Aisling demanded, Constance must have acquiesced, because Constance huffed and remarked that she would return in a moment. Bastion liked the nervous tremor in her voice when speaking of him. One booted foot stepped on the first stair on his descent and the room began to spin, spots filling his sight. A vision. Bastion knew it wasn't safe to stand, so just sat on the top stair instead and put his head in his hands and clenched his eyes shut, waiting. The flashes were stronger than ever, almost making him sway with each flash.

He embraced Aisling. The desire crashed into him like a bullet, but in his vision, she did not appear to feel the same. Was she crying? To slow the vision and get a better picture of the scene Bastion clenched his eyes together harder.

Out of nowhere an image of his brother and his nephew together at their home flashed. His brother's hand laid across his infant nephew saying that Niall was happy and content, then the vision disappeared in the mist.

"Mr. Guaire? Count Sueno? Are you quite alright?"

He opened his eyes to be greeted with the largest gray eyes he had ever seen. Aisling stood two stairs down level with his face and leaning in examining him. gently shaking his forearm.

"Yes, I–I just got dizzy. Must be all that time rumbling along in a carriage. Once on solid ground, my body has not yet fully recovered. I am quite fine thank you. No need for concern." He tried to dismiss his strange behavior but noted the intelligence that filled the pools of moonlight gray were not giving up so easily. She did however, back off and nod in acceptance of his story. She would be watching him though.

Rising from the stair they made their way to the entry hall's tiled floor.

"My sister Constance will be accompanying us as well."

"Wonderful. Glad to have the company."

"I have called for the gig to be brought around. It is much too far to walk from the house. We will take the gig into the pasture on the trail."

"Very well."

"Don't you need a notebook, or tools?" Aisling asked him. She obviously had done her reading about archeology, so he would have to be as careful as when on other expeditions with professionals.

"Oh, yes, I must have left them at the top of the stairs. I'll go back and collect them and meet you outside." taking the opportunity to get out from under her intelligent gaze for a moment more.

Returning to the entry hall just as a knock on the door heralded the groom with the gig. "Here we go." Aisling said to the little party and led the way to the small cart. Constance went directly to the bed of the wagon sitting against seat back of the bench and settled in again concentrating on a notebook.

Bastion's gentlemanly manners clashed with his decision to not speak up and offer her his seat. She seemed content after all.

He reached out a hand to assist Aisling up into the driver's seat, before moving around the back and hefting himself into the seat beside her. It was not a large buggy, making it unavoidable that their legs would brush with no room for either to give any space between them.

He caught Aisling's blush and knew from the warmth on his cheeks it mirrored his own. Even through two or more layers of clothes, who knew how many layers she had under her skirt, the heat and electricity surged into him. Perhaps a horse for his own use while in residence would be a wise choice, because surviving this torment every time they left to work may be more than anyone could take.

Aisling set the horse to a trot and they took off out across the lawn and into the field beyond. For an English day it could be counted as lovely. The sun however, didn't feel as warm this far from home.

Home. Those words swirled in his mind and pricked at a forgotten memory, or a vision, or, he wasn't sure, but part of him sensed home may not be as far as his travel dictated. The odd thought threw him, but it would have to wait. All Bastion's energy would be needed for the graveyard.

This would tell him if he was going to be able to assist Aisling and her sisters in their pursuit of clearing their family name. Aisling held certain her family to be innocent. However, not knowing exactly how much of the story she knew, and of that how much had been watered down over the years or changed to protect the family name from awful deeds, meant caution was paramount. Her family may well be responsible for the death of the neighbor's family member and thus no way to clear the Lightowler name.

The gig bumped along the horse trail, not made for a gig at all and kept slipping off the narrow trail to rumble along the rocky trail edge.

"Sorry, I know this must be horrible after such a long carriage ride."

"Nonsense, it is however making me not so despondent about the return trip. I will be thankful at every stop that the carriage is so well sprung."

Aisling laughed. as the sound light as the sunshine dancing in and out of the trees as they wobbled along. They were close enough to Scotland he was sure he heard a bit of a lilt when she spoke but certain her laugh had a Scottish edge to it. The sound washed over and calmed him, like nothing in recent memory. His muscles released from the tension of the ride, his desire, and the anticipation of a new search.

"You must find all this so strange." Aisling said as she maneuvered around a sharp corner, "Getting letters from a strange, unattached female asking you to come across two countries, and circumvent whatever military action is occurring at this moment."

"Well, I will say that it is not my usual correspondence." Bastion admitted.

"As I told you several times, I am a student of antiquity of sorts and therefore familiar with the work you have done on some of the digs you have been a part of."

"How, I must ask, does a young, gently bred woman such as yourself, become interested in archeology and antiquities?"

"I love history." She turned and smiled, lighting her big eyes and making them sparkle, "One day when we were at the lending library in the village, I came across a journal from the British Museum which had an article about the finds in Rome and I was captured. After that, I saved enough pin money to pay for a subscription, and I scour it front to back, and front again when I receive it."

Aisling spoke of history unlike any other woman. Most

women did not like his chosen vocation. Archeology tended toward the messy and dingy. Not to mention it kept him occupied. They did not like to discuss his interests at all, in fact they had instructed on many occasions to be more conversational in modern topics to keep them interested. He had the feeling that Aisling might very well get as dirty as any man on this job.

"Here we are. We walk from here, but you are probably very happy about that." She giggled, turned and bunching the billows of skirts in her arms, jumped from the gig to the ground. Bastion dismounted as well and waited while she tied the horse off and started up the trail.

"Are you not having your sister join us?" Bastion asked, with an edge to his voice. Just the thought of being alone with Aisling in the woods, sent a shot of heat through him, that should not be trusted. The vision on the stairs was some sort of warning and would need more consideration before making any move to seduce Aisling. Bastion refused to be the cause of her shed tears, visions be damned. "Oh, for the love of– Constance!" Aisling snapped, and the girl turned absentmindedly. "We have stopped, come along." Aisling directed with a gentler tone now that she had Constance's attention.

They waited for Constance to wiggle off the back and amble over to the make up the threesome. Still there was not attempt on her part to make eye contact or conversation. Had it been another person he might have thought them rude but recognized the concentration to art that it was. They walked in silence up the path. The sunbeams got fewer and the woods darkened. Under their feet the moss cushioned their steps, so the only noise the swooshing of the ladies' skirts around their legs as they stepped.

"We are very lucky to still have such thick woods. The king's men deemed the trees too small for ship making so they did not harvest them. I fear they will come back soon and use them anyway, but until then we enjoy them."

"I am surprised how lush it is in here."

As they trekked the sunshine peeked into the path ahead. "It is up here," Aisling said and picked up the pace. They stepped out into a small opening clearly an old burial ground. His skull began to tingle and the hair on his arms rose. The bones called to him. Disappointment welled that there was no time while solving Lightowler's dilemma to follow his curiosity.

"How many graves do you believe are here?"

" From what we can gather there are several, but there is one set apart from the rest that caught my eye." She pointed to the far corner of the open area to a marker.

"I thought you said you stumbled on this area, but it looks very well kept." Bastion asked confused.

"Oh, we did this." Aisling said swinging her arms to include the whole of the neat and tidy area.

"You cleaned this up by yourself? "Bastion asked, because if it had been as grown up as the area beyond them on the path, it would have been a monumental task.

"Yes, we did."

Bastion stepped across the space to the marker stone in question. It had a name and birth and death date carved into it, nothing more, however, the last name was scratched out for some reason Not that he expected more than that on a marker in the middle of nowhere in Northern England. touching the marker made the colors in front of him swirled. He could see a woman, tears streaming down her cheeks, painstakingly chipping away at the stone. Her grief palatable, anger mingled in the pain. It came as a sharp bitter taste in his mouth and an even sharper stabbing pain in his head just above his eyes. Bastion grabbed at his forehead to apply pressure. "Are you quite alright?" Aisling asked bending and setting a hand on his shoulder.

"Yes, perhaps there is some vegetation nearby that I do not like." To change the subject and because Bastion's instincts said this woman's story over reached making a burial marker he had to ask, "Are you sure there were no more markers? Not further in the brush around this area?"

"I couldn't say for certain, no, but we cleared until we came to this rock border. We assumed it a frame to the plot."

Bastion nodded but stepped passed the marker into the weeds to see for himself. "Tell me again, what has led to your current predicament. I have your letters but would rather have you retell it."

"Lord Landry, our neighbor to the east has wanted a plot of land that is part of the titled property. My father does not care to divide the property but has in the past told Lord Landry they welcome to use the land for grazing or even for crops."

"That is very generous of your father. We have similar agreements in Spain with our neighbors." Bastion cut in.

"Well, one would think so, but Lord Landry is not satisfied and has come up with this story of our ancestor being responsible for the death of one of the heirs to the Landry title and he has not been quiet about his allegations." Aisling stood ramrod straight and Bastion presumed this Lord Landry had not had the gull to say anything to her face about the situation.

"I see," Bastion said because the details would come out as they were needed and not before. Now the bones got their turn to speak.

CHAPTER 4

"There you are." Aisling heard Deidra call out from the library window as the small group approached the house after leaving the horse and gig at the stable and Bastion collecting his nephew and his nephew's tutor Perez. Aisling waved to her sister not wanting to yell in Senor Guaire's ear as they strode side by side up the lawn. Aisling however, wasn't certain Yelling would have any impact.

The Count had been silent since they left the little cemetery in the woods. She had not known what to say or how to spark up a conversation. They had virtually nothing in common.

Not that Aisling judged. A man like him would have some quirks and eccentricities. All the smartest of people did you see. Her father no exception to this. Papa was a veritable hermit, but people from all over England sought him out for his roses. Even Prinny had sent an inquiry about a new species.

But, Mr. Guaire and her Papa had little in common. Aisling got the distinct impression that she discomfited him. Just her. None of her sisters seemed to make him so uncomfortable. She sent him a side glance and realized he was chatting with Constance about the landscape and the statutes dotting the gardens. His face the epitome of relax gentleman even showing some enticing crinkles at the corners of his eyes. Senor Guaire had only offered the creases between his thick eyebrows, when they spoke. Aisling frowned at this and wondered why on Earth she would notice such a silly thing about a man.

"Papa has been looking for you," Deidra appeared, in Aisling's face. Aisling looked up surprised.

"Whatever for?" Aisling asked, not concerned in the least.

"He spoke with Mrs. Hascomb and found out about our new guests." Deidra answered with dread in her voice, "Papa is in a state, Aisling. I tried to calm him, but–."

Aisling had seen their papa livid before it wasn't anything she couldn't handle.

"Should we leave?" Bastion asked, concern clear for his nephew more than himself.

"No," Aisling assured him, "Papa will be fine. I am certain the two of you will have plenty to talk about once he calms enough to meet you. Excuse me."

Aisling didn't wait, she strode ahead of the group to confront him. They had argued about this, but she thought him resigned to the fact the family had to do something. Stalking through the house, not giving her eyes time to adjust to the dimness Aisling expected to bump into a table, but soon entered the openness of the entry hall and made a direct right into Viscount Lightowler's study.

"You were looking for my Papa?"

"What in the devil were you thinking making some poor sod travel the continent? Foolish girl."

Aisling was a lot of things, but they both knew foolish girl not to be one of them. Clearing her throat and squaring her shoulders this nonsense needed to stop. She loved Papa, but also Maria, Constance, and Deidra, and if something wasn't done soon, their chances for adequate matches would be dashed.

"Papa, I know how busy you are, but you also know how important this is. The Count wouldn't have traveled across a continent if he didn't think it possible."

"Baaa!" Viscount Lightowler's chosen word for when he won't win an argument but isn't happy about the outcome.

"You will meet him at dinner tonight. I think you will find him most interesting Papa, please give him a chance. You know Mama would not expect anything less."

"Yes, yes," Lightowler answered mollified, but not happily so. "I just think if you ignore the nonsense–"

"Papa it has gone past nonsense, and our non-response has people wondering if we are hiding because it is true, rather than thinking we are ignoring a falsehood. Maria has been uninvited to two events next month. Two, Papa," she waved a hand to indicate the world at large, and almost knocked over a large potted rose bush. Luckily, her father's back was turned, or the conversation would have taken a decidedly bad turn. "There are not enough families in the area to account for being unin-vited to two events. At this rate she may be forced to go stay with mama and our aunt to find a suitable match, and if that is so, who knows where poor Maria may have to go live. We may never see her again." Aisling knew making the threat that Papa's no action could force his youngest daughter to leave and never return would calm his ire for now."

"Humph. I still think you are wasting his time and money, but if this Count is fool enough to travel all this way, we might as well show him hospitality." The Viscount answered and turned back to his work bench.

Aisling put her hands on his shoulders, that were slumped down, to allow him to be close to the piece of rose bush he was working on and bent to kiss his jaw. Papa meant well, and loved his family, but she knew nothing could come between him and his roses.

Aisling left the study which was more like a laboratory and took in a deep breath. The thick heavy smell of roses in the closed space made it difficult to take in a full breath. The oxygen was cloaked in the cloying scent and made heavy in her lungs.

Deidra had been outside the door waiting, worry covering her face.

"You know if you don't stop you will have wrinkles long before I." Aisling stated marching passed toward the parlor to rest a bit before going to ready for dinner.

"Well?" Deidra asked, ignoring the barb.

"Papa is fine. He understands our urgency, doesn't think it is relevant, but understands it. Dinner will be as it always is."

"Good, I have not seen him in such a state in a few years. I thought he might kick Senor Guaire out before dinner." Deidra stated.

A pang shot through Aisling at the thought of Senor Guaire leaving. Unsure where that came from. She knew very little of him, only that available in the biography with his articles and what they exchanged in the letters. He like papa, in respect to speaking very little of himself unless pressed. As the sisters crossed the entry hall, Deidra turned away from the closed parlor door.

"I must check with cook that she does not need assistance, I also have some correspondence to attend to before evening."

"Very well. I will see you at dinner. Let me know if cook needs anything from me." Aisling offered and continued on to the parlor. It would be nice to just relax and work on needle work. Maria would be needing to finish the smocking on her new gown, so that would mean quiet company hopefully.

As she opened the door to the parlor the late afternoon sun shone through giving the room an inviting warmth. The large stuffed sofa held neither of the girls, however and to the left of the sofa a large form filled a quite substantial conversational chair. Aisling's heart thudded, and the sun filled room became uncomfortably warm, for her skin prickled with heat of its own.

"Mr. Guaire" was all she could manage. Stepping into the room, Aisling left the door ajar to keep things proper. "I assumed you would go settle your nephew in," she managed.

He rose in one fluid motion, that was both perplexing and fascinating. How could a man as large as him be more graceful than a woman? She did not look like that rising from a chair.

"My nephew was in need of a nap, and his tutor thought it best if they retire to the quiet of the room to do some reading." Waiting for Aisling to maneuver around the table and sit before resuming his own sitting position. "Perez seems to think that Niall is too active and animated when I am afoot." The warm smile on his face showed his love for the boy.

"Is Niall quite like your brother?" she asked

"My brother had been older by four years, so I have very few clear memories of him as a youngster, but I do see my brother in his son often."

"You miss him a great deal. I can tell. I do not know what I would do if I lost one of my sisters." Aisling mused, and they fell into a silence, not awkward per se, but not completely comfortable. She picked up her needlework and poked around the flower she had been working on for days, and Senor Guaire had a journal of sorts to study.

They continued to work each in their own world, but Aisling could not ignore his presence in the room and kept the conversation going.

"Are you familiar with the English seating for dinner?" Aisling asked trying to fill the silence. She never looked up from her needlework, but every once and a while could feel his stare on her.

"I am sure I can follow your lead." She looked up at the husky tremor in his voice not prepared for the strange glint in his eye. "Do you believe in destiny Miss Lightowler?"

"I ah, I believe that people are predetermined to follow a certain path. I do not, however believe that one cannot steer themselves away from the path." She answered, feeling the answer was very important at this juncture, but not sure why.

He rose and for a second, she thought he would come sit on the sofa, but instead moved around the chair and to a window to the right of the doorway at the mouth of the long room. "I do believe in destiny. My studies have shown me that people are pulled in one direction and disaster happens when someone fights or defies that pull."

"That is rather ominous Mr. Guaire." Aisling answered feeling a sadness seep into her bones. what could he have found in the cemetery? The needlework sat ignored, and Aisling rose to broach the distance between them. If bad news, she would rather he whisper it for some reason. Perhaps it would not be as bad on a whisper.

She settled a hand on his sleeve. "What is it Mr. Guaire?"

"Please call me Bastion. At least when we are alone." Aisling knew how a field mouse must feel under the scrutiny of a hungry cat. Senor Guaire's stare feral and hungry.

"I, well, it is a rather uncommon request between two people who know so little about each other." She was rambling.

Well, if you asked her sisters they would say every situation was a reason for Aisling to talk to excess. She did not agree with that estimation but was wont of anyone to side with.

"I would argue we know a great deal about each other after trading missives for almost a year." Bastion counted turning into her the slightest bit more. Aisling might be hard pressed to see it, but every cell in her body reacted to the movement. The hand she had offered still rested on his arm, and She now used it for leverage to sway the slightest bit closer to him as well.

Sitting down again would be the proper thing to do. His clean scent made her want to linger. "I do not believe we know enough to warrant first names." She said with less conviction than the words were meant to have.

"Please." And there it was. The one simple word that pushed her reserve off and settled them squarely into murky waters.

"very well I–" She swallowed her acquiescence looking again into his eyes and knowing at that minute she was about to be kissed and kissed very well. Glancing at the door, still open ajar. From where they stood anyone walking by would assume the room empty. All Aisling would only have to speak loudly, or step back into the view of the open door. She realized after a moment she had done neither of those things, and would not. Her body tingled from the tips of every strand of hair to the cramped toe in last year's slipper.

Bastion turned more fully and reached around to draw her near. The fleeting thought that she was going to kiss a man before his Christian name had crossed Aisling's lips faded. "Bastion" she heard herself say. More plea than statement, and with his name still vibrating on her lips he closed the space and bent to cover her mouth.

She should be shocked. She should stomp on his over large hessian and back away quickly. She should pull away and scream. Instead Aisling leaned in more fully and pushed up on tip toes. His lips were, oh Lord, his lips. They were firm yet soft and pliable. The feel of his smooth, soft, supple lips working her mouth to his desired position sent shockwaves through her body. He pulled back for a second, but in a very uncustomary move, Aisling's hands shot up to cup his face and pull it back to her mouth.

As if she had opened a flood gate, Bastion turned in one motion, never breaking contact and leaned her into the wall, putting them even more out of site. The hard wall pressed into her back giving the liquid bones structure, but his muscled body pressed with a softness that begged for more pressure. She let go of his face and wound both hands into his neck and the tie holding his too long hair back in a more acceptable style.

"Aisling" the sound wrenched from him on a growl. Aisling blinked up at this huge Adonis, who had engulfed her. She blinked again, trying to understand...well everything. What had stopped him? What drove him to kiss her? Why wasn't she surprised, or even shocked? He leaned in more but moved his hands away and instead rested his elbows on either side of her head and looked down at her. She barely came up to the top button of his waistcoat she thought distractedly drinking in the heat of him.

She looked up just in time to allow him to place a barely there kiss on her lips, that ended too quickly before leaving the room. Aisling stood against the wall acclimating back to Earth as the emptiness of the room engulfed her. Humming from anticipation and want she was not so young as to not under-stand why. This stranger had Come here and taken, no, not taken, her kisses were readily given. Why?

She walked back to the sofa and sat, picking up the forgotten needlework, only to absently let it rest in her lap instead looking out the window to the warm day. What did it say about a woman who would have willingly been ravished on the floor of the parlor? She should be appalled but wasn't. Desire flared and a vision of Bastion naked flashed. "Oh my." Aisling said to no one. The clock chimed the hour back the fact she needed to rest before dressing for dinner, but rest might well be unreachable. Laying in a bed with one's eyes closed would only bring back the kiss, which Aisling deduced would not be entirely restful.

Aisling decided she would have to figure out a way, because other women seemed to get through life after being thoroughly kissed so it would appear possible. Making her way to the door, she paused to stare at the once forgotten space by the window. It would now be an impossibility to ever enter or leave the parlor without looking right at that spot. Perhaps there would be more opportunity for Bastion to find more nooks and crannies in her old family house.

CHAPTER 5

he door behind him shut with a resounding thud, to which Bastion fell against it breathing like he had been chased. What just happened?

"Senor?" Niall's tutor came from the adjoining room concern clear on his face. Bastion chose his room for privacy, to calm this unrelenting urge to go back to the parlor and finish what they started. A five-year-old and his well-meaning tutor were not going to help him in his plight.

"I am fine, Perez, thank you."

"Are you sure? Would you like me to call for some tea?"

"No, I– I just need some time to rest before the dinner hour. You can close the door, so I don't wake Niall."

"Yes, Senor." He left, but with more concern than ever printed across his face. Bastion didn't care at the moment...

Making his way to the large bed, he fumbled with his cravat pulling it off and letting the stiff fabric fall hopelessly wrinkled to the floor, before falling into the bed.

What in bloody hell was he doing? Bastion laid on his back

with his arm draped over his eyes to keep out the afternoon sun and his surroundings. Coming here meant certain disaster. Life in Spain should be the priority. Not running toward the first positive vision he experienced in years. What a fool. A flash of Miss Lightowler between him and the wall sent heat from head to toe. How pliable she was. How soft. How untried. Bastion let out a long sigh. It would help immeasurably if she were averse to his advance, because his visions went well beyond some kissing in the parlor.

How could he help her when his visions seemed a jumble of his fantasy and reality? Were his visions were being compromised? This had never happened to him before.

Perhaps some tea and some food would help him. After ringing for a tray Bastion sat trying to sort the most recent visions. What did they mean? How would they be of help?

As Aisling, He felt certain it was a vision, because in his visions in Spain she looked as she did in the parlor just now after being well kissed. Delectable. Now it would take a herculean effort to not confuse his fantasy with reality. Visions are never about what you want, they are about what will be regardless.

Perhaps one of the other sisters could be persuaded help control the closeness and amount of time spent with Aisling. Yes, this plan had merit. The middle one, what was her name? Constance. Constance the dreamer. His mother had always blamed him for the very same thing, so he understood the featherheaded personality. The girl was thinking, always thinking. That one would be a good choice, but she would need to be dragged away from her sculpting. Bastion wasn't sure that possible. It seemed the others found that a difficult task.

Deidra the next in order to Aisling. Aisling and Deidra were close in age, perhaps only a year apart, but it seemed that

Deidra was in charge of the household in their mother's absence, or it could be Aisling and Deidra shared the load. She was far too busy to be pulled away, and he doubted she would feel as comfortable around him as Aisling. Another white-hot shot of desire tore through him.

Damn he wanted her. More than any other woman. Lack of experience had no bearing on this need. Bastion knew many women, it should be easy to curb his appetite for a fort night at the very least.

Deidra was a logical young woman he would just use a logical argument. The last and youngest sister could not be an option. He scared Maria. Just his size alone would intimidate some full-grown men, so to have a young woman, not much passed the age of majority, and not much taller than his elbow made sense.

Maria and Aisling were alike in stature, with Aisling only scants taller. He did not however intimidate Aisling and in fact met him kiss for kiss had him intrigued. Bastion spent most of his intimate life with older, more experienced women. Not that he desired them more, or less than women his age, but they were not as taken aback by his stature. Bastion could enter a ballroom, and know the approximate age of every woman, by how they reacted to his entrance. Women interested in Bastion's brand of attention were more confident with their own sexuality and knew what they wanted.

The food came, wasting no time to dive in he hoped by appeasing one appetite it would keep the other at bay. Thinking about food and going over the notes from earlier would lessen his thoughts of Aisling Lightowler. Perhaps stopping the throbbing in his head from his scheming to protect the woman.

With a piece of hard cheese, crusty bread, and some cold duck in one hand the journal in the other, Bastion sat at the writing desk next to the window. The breeze cool against his bare neck and reminded him to shave before dinner.

In his journal he began writing down his impressions both physical and supernatural while at the burial site. A chill ran through him, and though it was a cool time of day when they were there, this cold came from deep within. In his experience cold meant a bad death. At least one person in the plot did not die a pleasant death. The bone in particular, Aisling unearthed was cold, it also smelled heavily of something putrid, which also tended toward a violent dying. He had not gotten a clear vision however. It could be this bone and burial plot had nothing to do with her plight.

Bastion took a large ripping bite of the food and sat back considering this. Perhaps Miss Lightowler's very presence impacted the outcome of any experience. To have a non-tainted experience he would have to be there alone, but how to do that? A midnight trek may be needed. It would get him out of the house and perhaps his own head.

Satisfied with a possible plan he jotted down some other thoughts about the mystery woman, and questions he wanted answers to Finishing. A nap could not hurt before facing Aisling and her family, not to mention Viscount Lightowler at dinner. Controlling the visions easier with rest.

Bastion shimmied out of his coat and yanked off his tall hessians without needing to call Perez for assistance, which made him happy. The well sprung bed was a pleasant surprise. Staring up at the canopy He prayed for sleep to take him, before his thoughts turned to desire yet again.

∾

Bastion stood in a field, darkness obscured the landmarks, but a fire blazed in the distance. As lumbering toward the blaze, the smell hit him first, before the cheers of the people crowded around. I would appear the villagers were celebrating a festival, until the pyres came into view. They were burning people. To his horror, Bastion was witnessing three people being burned alive. Unseen by the cheering crowd one of the poor souls, not yet taken by the flames, looked up and made eye contact with Bastion. The contact so strong, the force pushed him back only to trip and fall onto the soft grass. The eyes looking back at him were the eyes he had looked at everyday in his childhood, that were filled with love, caring, and devotion. His mother's eyes.

Bastion woke in a cold sweat with the sheets twisted around his legs holding him to the bed, so tight, that trying to kick them off, only twisted them tighter forcing him off the bed with a thud, legs still trapped by the offending sheet now dangling from the mattress.

Perez came bursting through the door, "Senor, Senor, are you quiet, all right?"

"Yes, yes," Bastion grumbled, hoping that his fall from the bed, did not bring a bevy of servants, or worse Miss Lightowlers to see what conspired. "Help me will you, my leg seems to be caught."

Perez hurried over to free his employer's leg and after a moment gave Bastion a puzzled look.

"What?"

"Senor, these sheets are not simply caught up around your legs, they are tied." He said with a bit of confusion and a lot of concern in his voice.

"What? That can't be. I would never. There was no one in here. I just must have thrashed enough that is all. Get me out please." Bastion said not wanting to consider any other possibility.

"Yes, Senor."

In a matter of minutes, Perez had Bastion freed from his confines. Bastion thanked the tutor and asked him to call for someone to help him dress for dinner. As Perez left to do his bidding, Bastion went into his nephew's makeshift nursery to find him sitting on the floor playing with a whole box of wooden soldiers.

"Uncle, look what the nice ladies brought to me. They said while we are here they are mine to play with." Niall ran over to him and thrust one into Bastion's hand. It was well made, and kept in working order, with moving arms and legs.

"Well, that was very kind of them. I hope you said thank you." The boy frowned a bit "What is it?"

"I tried to say thank you, but Senor Perez had to do it for me. They did not understand me."

"Ah, yes. You do not speak English well yet. Perhaps this trip should serve as one large language lesson. I will speak to Senor Perez."

Unmoved, Niall was back to his toys. When he looked up at Bastion again, a pain shot straight to Bastion's heart. Looking back at him through the eyes of his nephew were indeed the eyes of the person burning in his dream. His mother's eyes. A chill snaked up his spine prickling the backs of his arms. Was his dream more of a warning? Should they leave at first light? had he put Niall in danger? Bastion didn't feel that the woman on the pyre warning him, more like welcoming him. What on earth did this have to do with the Lightowlers and their problems?

A noise from behind him brought him back to the bedroom, and the butler waiting to assist Bastion as they had discussed earlier.

"Thank you. I am sure this is not in your normal duties, to be the valet to any visiting guests." Bastion told Pilchard.

"Nonsense, Count Guaire. "Many years have passed, but I was His Lordship's valet when he was a young and about town. I do not mind assisting you in the least." Pilchard talked while choosing a deep gray superfine coat, and the deep blue satin waistcoat. Bastion would not have considered the two as a pairing but nodded more to himself than anyone in agreement. "If you are going to attempt to help fix this mess with His Lordship's family, I am more than willing to do my part."

"How much do you know about the circumstances, either today, or the original issue?" Bastion asked, since Pilchard offered.

"Well, what I can tell you of the current trouble, it was brought on by Viscount Landry and his son. They want the land to the east and are willing to spread horrible untruths to get it. They seem to think it the best way for them to get it. To shame the Lightowlers."

Bastion half expected to see the man spit on the floor at the sour taste of it all in his mouth.

"Well, I think that Lord Landry wants to sell the back pastureland to some developers, but Lord Lightowler owns the back pastureland and unwilling to either sell it outright or go into business with Landry." Pilchard went on as he took out a crisp new cravat from a drawer and began tying the thing is such an intricate knot, Bastion thought he might well have to cut himself out of it after dinner. "Mrs. Hascomb thinks it is because Lady Aisling snubbed Lord Landry's son at a local event and they took offense to it."

Bastion's smile slipped from his face. A knot formed in the pit of his stomach. Of course, Aisling had been courted, like any other English Lady of her age looking for a husband. A strange heaviness settled over him and Bastion decided not to dwell on the feeling or the thoughts about Aisling marrying.

"Is it not to your liking?" The butler come valet asked with concern.

"Oh, no I like it very well. I am just considering the options you laid on the table for what we are dealing with."

The butler snorted his disgust and moved to fastening the waistcoat and putting the fobs on as well. Bastion didn't believe that a country dinner warranted fobs, but he was new to the country, so would let the butler have his way.

Only after fully dressed he remembered his plan to shave. It was too late, dinner would be attended looking a bit gruff, so perhaps the fobs would make up the difference. thanking the butler, they planned for dinner tomorrow as well. He would not need assistance in the morning, Dressing in work clothing would not require a second set of hands.

Striding down to dinner, Bastion chewed on what Pilchard readily offered. Both were very petty to his mind, but from land disputes his brother dealt with, they could be very serious. However, a courtship issue with Aisling could send a man over the edge. It would not do to ask outright at dinner with the Viscount. Perhaps there was a way to work it into the conversation.

The butler was back in place at the dining room door to introduce him by the time Bastion rounded the corner from the stairs.

"You move well." Bastion complimented just as the butler announced him, and Bastion caught the smile at the corner of his mouth.

Bastion entered the room. All seemed to be present except Aisling. Had he so traumatized her she couldn't be seen in public? Deidra made the introductions between her father and Bastion well enough.

"Papa, I would like to introduce you to our guest. This is Count Guaire, fourth Count of Lugar De Sueno. Count Guaire, this is my papa Viscount Lightowler."

"Please My Lord, call me Bastion. I am very new to the title and it does not feel as if it fits yet."

"Yes, well very good meet you." The Viscount said and shook hands with Bastion. "I am afraid my daughter dragged you across the continent for no good reason. I do not think it of great circumstance. At lease not as much as my daughters do." He continued looking around.

"Where is Aisling?" Lightowler asked looking at the other girls who were all standing waiting to be allowed to sit.

"You know Aisling papa," Maria answered, but looked under thick blond lashes toward Bastion as if he might bite.

"Maria." Deidra chastised her sister, "I am sure she will be here in a moment. I sent Mrs. Hascomb to see if she required assistance. I would suggest we start the soup course, so it will not cool over much."

Viscount Lightowler nodded in agreement, and the girls took their seats following the gentlemen. Just as the soup was being served a whoosh sound came through the door.

"I am terribly sorry. Terribly so." A winded Aisling apologized as she hurried to the table and took the seat next to Deidra across from Bastion, without waiting for either gentleman to rise. Lightowler, however did not look up from his soup, so Bastion got the impression Aisling missed the opportunity to see gentlemanly manners from her father for the evening.

"I am terribly sorry." Aisling said looking directly at Bastion.

With only a hint of a pink blush. which could easily be dismissed as the exertions needed to get to dinner before the entre was served Bastion gave her points for having such nerve. He would blame the temperature of the soup if pressed on his blush, but just seeing Aisling with color in her cheeks, and dark hair dancing in little curls around her face kicked up his temperature.

"It is of no consequence. dinner at my brother's table was difficult for me to keep. I was testament to his patience."

"Why?"

"I often I had gotten engrossed in a journal or article, or some such thing and lost count of time." He admitted, feeling nostalgic, thinking about his brother's face when Bastion would join the dinner, much like Aisling just had. The memory made him smile. "Louis was perplexed and often said with my size it was a wonder they were able to keep food in the larder, so for me to be late for meals seemed a bit of a conundrum."

Everyone laughed, Maria even relaxed a bit with him referring to his own size. The table quieted as everyone set to eating. As the courses were changed Deidra started the conversation.

"Count Guaire, how did your nephew care for the soldiers?"

"Oh, quite taken by them thank you, but I do have to convey Niall's distress in requiring a translator to express his thanks." Bastion chuckled. "I have told him that while we are in England I will instruct his tutor to use it as a large lesson in English speaking."

"Oh, Niall is a sweet boy," Deidra commented.

"You should go spend time with him Deidra, you speak Spanish very well," commented Maria.

"You speak Spanish?" Bastion asked surprised. French would be expected, but Spanish would not be as necessary for an English Lady.

"She does," answered Aisling. "She will not boast about

herself, so we have to I am afraid." Deidra and Aisling returned glances, that Bastion understood as a sibling. "Deidra speaks French, Dutch, Spanish, and German."

This impressed Bastion. "Most women I am acquainted with know two perhaps three, but I am not sure I have every made the acquaintance of a woman or gentleman for that matter that speaks four languages outside of their own."

"Thank you." Deidra said with a pretty blush staining her cheeks. She bent to pay attention to the buttered potatoes, when Aisling spoke up.

"Yes, she is in search of a young clerk, or solicitor, and believed it would only be of help to know any language that a future husband may need to know."

Deidra gave Aisling a look that would have silenced a lesser woman, but Aisling only laughed. "We are very proud of her. She is much too intelligent to waste away in the country and will make a marvelous match for a man that deserves someone so special."

"So Guaire," cut in the Viscount, with no seeming understanding that there were other conversations afoot. "Do you like roses?"

"Yes, My Lord I do enjoy roses. We have many roses lining the perimeter of our home, most, however near where my mother lived. She enjoyed having the blooms fill the house with scent while they were blooming.

"I will have to show you my garden and my workshop. Working on a new variety for the Regent, you know."

"Ah, yes, Aisling mentioned that in our correspondence."

"Papa, I am afraid Count Guaire will be busy. He is here for a purpose. We wouldn't want to waste his time."

"Pah!" The Viscount swished the idea out of the air. "This boy will get more from learning about my roses than walking through the forest digging up bones. You girls have already wasted his time."

"I wouldn't have come had I not thought I could help, My Lord." Bastion assured the family as all the girls stiffened at their father's declaration. "But, I would also be very interested in learning about your roses and your work. I am sure as the days are long, I can manage both endeavors." Bastion caught Aisling's glance and winked. Making her smile, before glancing around to check if anyone saw the interaction.

"Well, you are welcome to dig anywhere you like except my rose garden. That land has been tilled and re tilled, nothing there except chicken droppings and tea leaves in that soil."

"Of course." Bastion agreed. "I have seen where Aisling would like me to concentrate. Do you have any other suggestions? You know more about your family history I am sure."

The viscount looked up from his roast pork staring hard at Bastion. After a few moments, "Well, if you must be here to justify your travels, there is an old stone foundation about a mile north west of that site Aisling showed you. According to my family documents building in question was in the center of the first dispute."

"Dispute?" Bastion asked, hoping to coax more from him.

"Well, from what my records indicate and from hearing stories as a boy, that was once the manor house, before they built this one. In a much better location than this home, but something happened, and it was destroyed."

"What happened Papa?" Constance, who had been silent the entire meal asked with rapt interest at her father's story.

"Pah!"

"Please papa." Constance asked again, and with a coy smile and a nod, her father started speaking. Bastion got the impression his middle daughter could charm anything from the viscount and the other girls knew it as well, as they all shared small yet discernable smiles.

"Nothing but fodder for one of those gothic novels Maria is so keen to read." Lightowler grumbled.

"Papa!" Maria protested turning a bright shade of pink.

"If you must hear a version, better it be mine I guess." He put a large piece of pork in his mouth, put his fork down and sat back chewing heartily. "It was near eighty years ago or more. My mother remembered it clearly, it was her aunt you see. Lady Corinthia. The oldest daughter to the then Viscount Lightowler. Had she lived I may not have inherited the title." Lightowler shifted draping one long leg over the other, settling in to tell his story.

"Lady Corinthia had a grand love for the local first son of the then Viscount Landry. The bans had been read and as a bride price and a gift to Lady Corinthia, Lord William, the groom gave her the northern parcel of land and the manor house. The property became part of the Lightowler estate, but the manor house was to remain Corinthia's and William and Corinthia were set to live there once they were married."

Bastion knew the basics as Aisling had given them to him, But Lightowler may have new information that would help lead him in a more direct direction. Bastion had the feeling that his answers would not lie in the graves.

"It got out that when Lady Corinthia heard about the unborn child of William to a servant girl she was devastated, but still wanted to go through with the wedding. I have a journal that states as much. She had not yet moved all her belongings to the manor house you see. There were still a few boxes remaining with here."

New information abounds. "Journal? You say you have it?"

"Well yes. It doesn't say much but does state she loved him and wanted to make a go of the marriage."

"Might I borrow it? It might help me to ah, get better into her mindset."

"I don't see why not. I'll have Mrs. Hascomb dig it out for you."

"Thank you."

"Papa finish please." Constance prodded.

"Very well. According to accounts, William got a note, found in his rooms after the fire, from Corinthia asking him to meet at the manor house for a romantic meeting before the wedding and to reconcile. "The older man bent over and took his fork and spent a moment digging some pork out of his tooth and resumed. "He was heard running from the Landry house toward the fire yelling to get the water brigade.

"When the fire finally burned itself out, there were three sets of bones found. On two of the fingers William's signet ring and Corinthia's emerald engagement ring. On the other set of bones, a cross necklace was found partially melted into the sternum. It was believed to be the servant girl who was pregnant with William's child. However, all but the signet went missing long ago."

Bastion sat in the silent room. Apparently, the girls were hearing this for the first time. Aisling never mentioned anything about a mistress or baby. The Viscount snorted at the stunned looks.

"Pah, see I told you a gothic novel. Nonsense. If you ask me."

"You don't believe it happened?"

"I don't believe it happened the way the Landy's have been trying to spin it for years and now adding to it that Corinthia had plans to kill them both and make it out alive is preposterous."

"How so?" Bastion asked hoping for just a bit more information before his new acquaintance decided he had said too much.

"Because," waving his arms in the air as if it should be plainly clear to all idiots. "Lady Corinthia was found as far from the entrance to the house as one could be. There was no way out from there. Clearly, she had no intentions of getting out alive. As for if she planned a murder suicide I have no idea, and really feel that it was a crime and a story for another time. It has no bearing on our modern family."

And with that he was done. Lord Lightowler pushed the rest of the way from the table and excused himself before the dessert course.

Bastion needed to get his hands on that journal and needed to go to the manor house rubble. Alone. At least a better place to begin than where Aisling had him looking earlier.

CHAPTER 6

The next morning at the breakfast table, Bastion sat dressed in his field attire, which was not suitable for polite table manners, but it seemed a waste of everyone's time for him to ring for a tray If he ate quickly enough he could be gone before the rest of the household rose.

And just for good measure there would be no time for a second cup of coffee. Bastion asked the night before if cook would do up a basket of luncheon items and ale for his day. Another way to avoid running into Aisling not returning to the house until late. If there was no chance to see, hear, smell, or Lord help him, taste her the temptation would be silenced. In his mind, if he got as far as tasting, his plight would be lost for sure remembering her honeyed lips from their previous encounter.

Snapping his head up at footfalls, Bastion let out a breath when Constance entered the room. Taken up short by his presence Constance stopped in the doorway, but did not notice his attire, or not enough to be affected.

"Good morning, Miss Lightowler. I trust you passed the night well?"

"Good morning, Count Guaire. I slept very well, but I always do." Constance answered heading to the sideboard and filling up a plate with ham eggs, and potatoes. She sat across from Bastion and dove into her food with ambition.

"Are you late for an appointment?" Bastion asked, taking the last bite of his own meal and pushing the plate away.

"No, well yes," She tried to answer around a large piece of ham and egg. "I need to get to my studio. I have a marvelous idea for a new statute, and I want the morning light as I begin."

"A true artist. I admire you," Bastion complimented. "My mother was an artist, she sensed what the canvas wanted and could bring it life."

"Really? You do not strike me as creative." Constance said dryly. Bastion knew she meant no insult. The middle daughter similar to the Viscount. The world was her art, his roses. Anything beyond that not of concern. Neither had the time for the tact and interplay of modern conversation. Bastion smiled. He quite liked both Constance and Viscount Lightowler. With both you would never have to wonder where you stood with them.

"No not over much." Bastion admitted. "My mother was very disheartened by both my brother and me for that reason. We are both much more like my father. I, according to my brother am much more like my mother in that I am un sonador. How do you say? A dreamer?"

Constance chuckled at that and nodded, but kept to her task of eating diligently, until she scooped up the last of the potatoes and drained a cup of fresh goat milk. "I wish you luck today, Count Guaire. I hope Papa gave you better direction."

"I he did. Thank you, and good luck to you. Perhaps I will

still be in residence when you have the essence of your sculpture set."

Bastion rose as she trotted out of the room, dressed similarly to himself–for hard, dirty, labor some work.

Bastion left as well managed to make his way to the kitchen, then out to the gig that had also been requested last night be ready for him. The sun had not yet peaked over the edge of the lawn, but the stray pinks and yellows of it on the horizon heralded its arrival.

As Bastion led the horse into the woods he hoped that this new site would bring some better information. The burial site may be helpful, but not until there further evidence and know better what to look for.

The forest air hung cool in the dimness. The horse seemed to know the way as they both plodded along the path toward the foundation plot. Bastion liked being the first one to a site. His hands tingled with anticipation. His mind swirled with questions about what he would find there.

As the horse rounded a turn the forest opened to what the Viscount had called the north pasture. A large open space, and Bastion could see its worth to developers. It was flat and would require little in the way of preparation for any building endeavor. The sun we just cresting the horizon and the entire field sparkled as the sunbeams played off the morning dew like diamonds in candle light. As the gig continued, Bastion's entire right side began to tingle. The hair rose and danced, sending chills along his side.

Bastion learned over many years of coping with his gift that you went where you were directed About a quarter of a mile down the field the rubble foundation stuck up like a scar on the landscape. Bastion stopped and surveyed the scene.

After emptying his tools, notebook, and basket of food the

horse got tethered to a shady area. The quiet of the morning appealed to Bastion as he went and stood in the middle of the structure. Not very much of the original structure still stood, and surprisingly, nothing had grown around or in its foundation. Almost as though waiting but waiting for what?

With no sign that anyone had been near the site for some time Bastion made his way to the edge of the stone outline and took a seat. Taking off his gloves and laying them on the ground not forget to grab them later and laid a hand on the stone that would have held up the entrance frame. Like a water spout being opened all at once Bastion overflowed with visions, emotions, smells, colors. He yanked his hand away as if burned.

"Damn" his fingers tingled. "You have much to say, but you cannot say it all at once." He said to the rocks. Bastion did not believe they would listen, but it made him feel in control. drawing in a long deep breath, and gingerly placing just his fingers on the rock next to him ready this time the intensity was less than before and Bastion could sort to some extent the sensations flooding him.

It was night. The smell of roast meat and wild garlic filled the clearing. Dinner. The warmth of love stretched up his arm and into his chest. Warm and tight around his arm. This a place of love, for love at one time. A young woman, Corinthia perhaps, hummed as she set out flowers. The emerald ring glinted off the fire light, yes Corinthia. No sense of unhappiness and no angry or fear came from her

Bastion noted. To his left came a cold chill. Walking passed him and through the door a woman, heavy with child. She had a bag that smelled of oil and gun powder? This young woman radiated hatred. It came off her in waves of red and black. They encircled her like a great storm. Smoke, Bastion tasted it first, next seeing the flickering of flames and smelling the thick heavy smoke of old wood burning. It coated his throat making him cough. It filled his nostrils and made his eyes burn. A wave of fear washed over him. It came crashing into him almost knocking him from the stone. White hot fear. A man appeared dressed in the height of fashion eighty years ago, once through the door the stranger stood yelling, but Bastion could not hear or make out any words.

All at once Bastion was inside the burning home with the man. "Mary, what have you done? For the love of God, what have you done?" The man in white hot fear yelled. Bastion looked in the direction of his pleas and saw the angry woman lying on the floor, pregnant belly distended from the weight of the unborn child, a slow trickle of blood becoming larger at the top of her chest. The pull to try and save the child ripped through his chest, just as the screams rang out. Screams of fear and pain.

The man's color changed to a cloudy gray with swirls of red. He could not save them both. Save a baby that might not live, and would have the designation of bastard his entire life, or save his betrothed? A ball of guilt settled in Bastion's stomach like the guilt of the man for putting them all at this spot at this moment. Racing after the man wending his way through the growing thickening smoke, but when they reached the woman, she had collapsed on the floor, flames licking the long skirts and just as the man would have reached for his love to drag her to safety the ceiling gave way knocking the him back into the hall. Both Bastion and the distraught fiancé stood silent in shock of what they both knew had just happened. The man's color swirl turned a deep purple with red and black swirls.

He strode back down the hallway but stopped at the top of the long staircase and sat down. His knees curled into his chest and his head bent resting on his knees waiting for the blaze to take him. He would not live a life worth living without his betrothed or his child. He would not, and he could not.

~

Aisling watched Bastion from the gig with rising panic. She had been just crawling out of bed, when something caught her eye out of the bedroom window. Hurrying to dress and ready to not miss him, but at the cost of her hair and choice of morning gown. Looking down at Aisling realized she donned two different styles of half boots. It was all worth it for this moment though.

Not sure what Bastion was doing, but not wanting to disturb him, she had nestled against the gig and waited. The large man sat on the ruble staring off. The longer he sat the heavier his breathing got. The breeze rustled her skirts and swirled the wildflowers around, but Bastion didn't pay any heed. Aisling watched as his expression changed. Anger? She couldn't tell and didn't understand why his mood changed.

She needed to be closer and slinked up behind him, but Bastion paid no heed. His face shone red with small droplets of sweat forming on his brow and he was shaking. It might well be some sort of fit. Having read about such a thing, she knew not leave him alone. Should he be woken though? Did one call it woken if they are not actually asleep? Would that make it worse?

Her need to act overrode concern for jarring him too much and reached out grabbing his upper arm. And for a moment she was taken aback by the fact that her hand all spread out didn't even span his arm to allow her fingers to curl around it on either side. Lord he was large... and well-muscled. No wonder a woman's hand made no impression to bring him back.

She shook him, "Count Guaire. Count. Bastion. Wake up." She shook harder and moved in closer. Whatever had his mind, it wasn't letting him go. Shaking his head at something Aisling could not see. It became apparent more drastic action had to be taken. "Bastion. Bastion. Are you quite well?" speaking louder and shaking harder had no effect. Just when she thought all lost he took in a great breath and flailed his arms. The motion sent him backward off the rock knocking her off balance in a flurry of skirts.

Bastion sat up first looking around until his view lighted on Aisling. She managed to bring herself up on her elbows only to realize too late it had been struck in the fall, and the pain shot up one arm and down into her wrist making all the fingers tingle. She grabbed at the offending arm.

"What are you doing here?" Bastion asked rising and stepping over the crumbling foundation to help Aisling up. "Let me see." grabbing the bent arm to examine the bruised elbow.

"It is fine, I just bumped it." She assured him, not feeling comfortable about Bastion's examination, even just her elbow.

"I am sorry," She said tersely. "I didn't mean to disturb you, but I thought you might be having–" cutting herself off. How does one suggest another is not right without being insulting? Mama would know, but that was not going to help now.

"Having what?" he asked, apparently satisfied. "Well, since I do not have the vocabulary to be more polite, I thought you were having some sort of an episode or fit."

She waited for him to turn in horror or to have some sort of reply, but he grunted and just kept staring at the foundation.

"Did you hear me?" She finally asked walking over to him to try and see what held his attention.

"What? Yes, I heard you. I am fine I assure you. Hand me that shovel." He pointed in the direction of a pile of tools and leather satchels laid next to the edge of the foundation. She stomped over grabbed the shovel and returned with it.

Bastion ambled over to a spot, looked around at nothing as

far as Aisling could see and began digging. She stood on top of the foundation for a better vantage point. Only after a few moments Bastion's shovel came up with something. A fabric of some sort. As soon as it came out of the ground and the fresh air hit it Aisling covered her nose and mouth. Mixed in with the smell of rotting cloth and freshly over turned dirt was the rancid smell of oil or some sort of accelerant.

"What is that?" Aisling asked jumping off the rock, her face still covered.

"I believe a pack or satchel of some sort." Bastion replied. Setting the shovel down, he picked leather gloves off the ground and donned them before reaching down and carefully plucking up the fabric. In great disrepair it would not be long before the earth took it back. Bastion turned the fabric over in his hand and Aisling saw something on the front.

"What is that?" She asked pointing over Bastion's shoulder smiling at the annoyed glance she received from him. after wiping at the spot with his glove it appeared to be a metal plate of some sort, still connected by a fastener to the fabric. As he wiped more it became obvious there was something stamped into the metal, but the dirt builds up made it almost impossible to read.

"Bring me that jug." pointing in the direction of the pile of supplies again.

Aisling retrieved the jug and slowly poured ale over the metal plate as Bastion held the fabric with care not to tear the delicate fibers. The ale only seemed to make the smell worse, but with a swipe or two of his leather covered thumb the words Landy Stables est. 1717 shone brightly all cleaned.

"What does this mean?" Aisling asked trying to understand if this was a clue or just an artifact.

"I am not sure just yet." draped over his shoulder. "I am fine here alone. You do not need to remain. I am sure–"

"I don't mind. I have nothing pressing." Aisling spoke up, cutting him short certain that sounded much too much like a desperate woman. She had been so nervous before dinner and almost didn't attend, but at the last moment schooled her features and what a lady would do. All went fine, she supposed. No one at the table seemed to sense anything untoward. She however, spent the entire meal feeling almost itchy nerves vibrating at every glance, deep voiced comment, or heaven help her mistaken touch when both tried to reach for the salt bowl at once. the whole business so unsettled Aisling that when she retired to bed, sleep was almost impossible, and any fitful sleep Aisling did have kept reliving their encounter in the parlor. Rising before luncheon had been a feat of fortitude, now she was being dismissed?

"I find this sort of thing fascinating. I would not have found you if not for my interest in history and the search for artifacts. I assure you I will endeavor to stay out of your way, if you allow me to remain." That was as good an excuse as any to remain she thought.

Bastion stared at her with a hard look but must have decided the plea in earnest, because he grunted again and turned back to his work.

"This is so exciting. Does that happen often that you find something the first place you dig?" She asked pressing past the awkward moment following behind him strolling more into the center of the space. "This must have been a very large manor house." She thought out loud. Looking around.

A wall of muscle halted any forward movement. Bastion had stopped, and she had not, looking off to the left and not in front of her. She stepped back to put some space between them. "Oh, I am sorry."

"I thought you said you would observe and not be in the way?"

"Well, technically, you were just in my way. You didn't walk into me." She pointed out.

turning sharply to confront her, Aisling's breath caught. He was mere eyelash strands away and the sun, now firmly planted in the sky for the day sent beams of muted light across his dark, tanned face illuminating his eyes. If Aisling looked long enough she might just fall into the soft pools of honey brown swirls with little green flakes.

Whatever set down sat on his tongue never came, instead they stood facing off. In that moment, Aisling realized they were different. She knew their meeting was going to leave them both changed forever, but how? Already having dealt with rejection on a very public level would it not hurt as much if it remained private between two people? She doubted it. It might hurt worse. Running a much better option. Her feet remained planted in the spot.

After what seemed like eons, Bastion straightened and cleared his throat. "About yesterday—"

"No need." Aisling spoke up. She did not want to hear him say it was a mistake, or he shouldn't have made an advance. He shouldn't have, but that doesn't mean it wasn't welcome. This Spaniard affected her, and she would not allow that to be cheapened. An ache began to throb.

"No, there is a need." Bastion interrupted. "Here I am a stranger, come into your home. You haven't even had a chance to get to know me or I you. It is a wonder and a testament to your manners that my whole contingent was not kicked out immediately. What?" He obviously saw every emotion stark on her face. Aisling's emotions did not hide well, she might as well not waste their time.

"I am just- just happy you didn't say you shouldn't have done it."

"Well-" rubbing the back of his neck in a nervous way.

"Don't you dare. Unless is the unpleasantness of it is too much to bear, then by all means please tell me." She said and watched his face lift as he laughed. Laughing was good wasn't it?

"No, Aisling it was not unpleasant. I assure you of that. I could spend an entire afternoon doing that with you." reaching up to tuck a curl behind her ear. Heat from his hand warmed her. Oh Lord!

"I know I must sound like a horrible person, or at least a very wonton woman. I assure you, I am not." She tried to explain, but she looked up into his eyes and the words died on her tongue. His hand still hovering by one ear settled at the nape of her neck and gently tugged toward him as she bent up to meet his kiss.

The warmth from the sun was not enough to keep the chills at bay. They started it at his touch and wound like ribbon down filling her with shivers. She leaned into his body wanting to absorb the heat radiating from him. The few pins she managed to lodge in to hold the mass of hair at bay with no help from a maid did not do their job. They fell to the ground in silence. He pulled away from the kiss panting heavily, but not letting go. "Aisling" and he dipped his head below her face and spread kisses around her neck and down along the neckline of her dress.

Aisling wasn't sure where it came from, but a moan escaped as she leaned back more into his palm to give him better access. His other hand still gloved slid up the side of the dress and came to rest over one breast. The skin and nipple puckered under her chemise and the pressure from his hand sent devilish waves to her belly.

Bastion stilled. Aisling's eyes fluttered open to see him looking into the woods. Listening.

"Wha–"

"Shhh"

Aisling listened as well and didn't hear anything until the crack of a twig broke the morning silence. Bastion's embrace ceased as if she were on fire and stepped several feet away. To her credit, Aisling did not stumble backward and land for the second time today on the ground. Side stepping and picking up the shovel that lay next to her feet she began poking around in the dirt. No longer looking into the woods, not wanting to rise suspicion when Bastion yelled.

"What the– Oh, damn it!" he said as she looked up and saw him walking backward with his hands raised in supplication.

Aisling turned to see a huge gray, lanky, four-legged form emerging from the trees. She looked over at Bastion and determined he thought the beast fierce and dangerous. Sighing heavily, knowing that the animal would not be alone, she would have to brace herself for the now imminent meeting.

"Bennett. Bennett down!" Aisling commanded the huge Irish Wolfhound owned by Lord Landry's son. The dog was quite a love if he deemed you worthy, but she could see where a person who had not been properly introduced would be intimidated. The dog's back stood well past her waist and could easily look Aisling in the eyes. Bennett appeared shaggy, but upon further inspection his hair tended toward coarseness closer to his body and almost wispy on the fringes. She had to smile at how someone as large as Bastion kept backing away slowly, but Bennett moved faster and in one great leap, flopped his huge paws on either side of Bastion's chest and began licking.

Aisling couldn't help it and laughed out loud. she did manage a chastising "Bennett get down!" before the giggles over took her and she had to use both hands to silence them.

"Bennett is it?" Bastion asked, she nodded. "Bennett my boy, good perro, ah, dog. Good dog." He tried to say between swipes of the tongue. "Now get down."

Bennett didn't listen and continued licking Bastion until Aisling got a hold of herself and yanked the great beast from Bastion with both hands and much of her weight. The leather collar didn't do much in the way of keeping Bennett tethered to anything, but it could be used as a handle.

"Bad dog Bennett, now sit." And the dog harrumphed, but sat dutifully, wagging his tale and panting. "Good boy."

"What might I ask is a Bennett?" Bastion asked busy drying his face and neck from all the love.

"Bennett is Lord Landry's son's prized Irish Wolfhound." Aisling answered, looking warily around them for the son. He would not be far behind. "We should leave. At once."

"Whatever for I am just–"

"Because, I should not be seen alone with you, without a chaperone."

Bastion's expression said everything.

"I know, I should not have come after you. Lesson learned but let us not make the situation worse by being found out." She said, grabbing her skirts and heading for the trail back to her house.

"I cannot leave the gig, horse, and all my tools. You go, and I will catch up."

"But–"

"Go." Bastion said as they both heard shouts for the missing

Bennett coming from the other direction. Aisling would have liked to argue but didn't want to add fuel to the already social disaster that was the family's reputation right now and Landry would not wait a moment before passing that along to interested parties. She didn't go as far as the house though, turning down the path and doubling back to make sure Bastion handled Landry and not the other way round. He could be an insufferable bore, but Aisling assumed Bastion's size alone would curb Landry a bit or, so she hoped.

CHAPTER 7

"*B*ennett! Damn it all Bennett where the bloody hell have you gone off?"

Bastion heard the calls for the dog and looked down. The beast did not appear swayed in the least by the calls or the profanity. He continued to sit and in fact let out a huge yawn showing a full set of large white teeth. "It's a damn good thing you are good natured." Bastion commented to the dog who looked up at him and blinked, all the while still wagging his tale.

After another few moments an Englishman stepped out into the clearing with a look of surprise on his face to see his dog sitting well behaved next to a complete stranger.

"I say, that is my dog." The gentleman commanded.

"I assumed as much when I heard you calling. Large enough beast, isn't he?" Bastion asked, he might as well see what this Brit knew of what was going on. "A good hunter?"

"The best, when he doesn't run astray." The gentleman answered walking up to the dog and being greeted with a bigger tail wag and panting. "His damn nose gets him every time. Once he gets some age on him, Bennett will come to tow."

"I wasn't sure if he was friendly or not when he came bounding out of the woods at me."

"What is that accent?"

"Spanish. Count Guaire." Bastion held out his hand. The other man accepted well enough.

"You are a long way from Spain, Count. I'm Landry. What brings you to the forests of Northern England?" the two men shook hands.

"History." Bastion answered. "I am a historian. I am traveling the continent looking for interesting stories and the like. Do you know of any?"

A strange glint filled Landry's eyes and Bastion knew he had struck a nerve.

"As a matter of fact, I do, about this very place we are standing."

"Really? Would you be willing to share it?" Bastion asked digging into his bag and pulling out a notepad and a pencil. Landry was more than happy to dive into the story of unrequited love, with Corinthia being the villain and planning his death and her subsequent suicide, for according to his version, she was quite mad.

"Is there any proof?" Bastion asked when Landry had exhausted his list of reasons the entire Lightowler family had taken on the same madness. Landry stared at Bastion. Bastion assumed he had not expected a complete stranger to ask for proof. Perhaps no one in town had bothered to check the story.

"Well, of course I have proof. One doesn't just go around calling down an entire family without proof." Landry said with a good amount of insult in his voice. Bennett had laid at Bastion's feet. If making a run for it was necessary Bennett would trip him up. Bastion hoped the expression he sported was one of interest and not suspicion. Bastion wanted objectivity after all. A chance remained that the Lightowlers didn't have all the facts straight. He doubted it but needed to strive for objectivity just the same. "Well, obviously I don't have it with me."

"Oh, of course. I wouldn't think that you would." Bastion quite liked the young Lord Landry and fought the jealousy welling up in his stomach. Under different circumstances they could get on well as friends. It also wasn't clear if this was the dastardly black guard Aisling painted him to be. He thought about Aisling's very practical manner and wondered at her strong feelings. Did he spurn her? Did Aisling have stronger feelings for him than he knew? Bastion did not like the energy coursing through his body at that thought.

"Well, Lord Landry it was a pleasure, but I am afraid I need to pack up and be on my way to check on my nephew. Perhaps we will run into each other another time and we can continue our discourse."

"Yes, yes let's. It is advantageous that we met. I get bored by the lack of diversity of people in the country. The same faces with the same stories over and over. I would very much like to get to know you more."

The men shook hands, Landry got the great giant of a dog in tow, at least for the time being and they headed back off from where they came. Bastion did have to get back to clean off his find and to see if the journal that Lord Lightowler had promised had been found and delivered to his room yet. Now, Bastion was getting quite excited about learning the outcome of this story that seemed to be unraveling and changing with every person involved. By exuding caution, perhaps avoiding Aisling could be accomplished.

"Well, that was unpleasant." Came a soft, feminine voice from behind him. Bastion froze. Perhaps if the goal indeed was to avoid Aisling he should simply stop thinking about her, because that seemed to conjure the woman, whenever a stray thought passed through his mind.

"I thought you went back." He said resuming his packing.

"Heavens no. I just didn't think it prudent to let Landry see us alone. Together. In the woods."

He continued to pick up his things turning his back on her.

"Well, what are you doing?" She asked coming up behind him. perfume wafted over his shoulder, filling his head with the smell of lavender and lemons. And with that the world shifted. His head filled with pressure like it would explode.

The shovel in his hand dropped to the ground seconds before he joined it. Hoping to lessen the spinning Bastion grabbed his head. Like in a large room, Aisling's voice asking if he was quite unwell echoed far away. Allowing the vision to have its way the only way to get passed this.

Flashes of milky white skin and shimmers of fine lace flashed like the flickering candle. Gooseflesh rose where ever she touched. A long leg wrapped around his naked hip. Her taste filled his senses. She was every decadent pastry he had ever sampled, and Bastion would never get his fill. "My Love." *He heard himself whisper.*

Oh, Lord no. To love Aisling would prove disastrous. She deserved more, but the vision persisted. *They were in a field, she was smiling and laughing at something his said bending her head up to see his face more fully, and there in her eyes the love returned. His destiny and his family. He bent down and laid a kiss on her lips, they tumbled to the ground as one, but the landscape again changed, and they were in his bedchamber still embracing.*

Bastion could not stand it anymore and ripped his eyes open, cutting the connection to whatever force caused him to see those things that were better off not seen. He sat panting, grasping to gain his breath and bring him back to the present. His head still spun and tingled from his exertions. This headache would persist for some time for forcing himself out of the vision. Aisling had a right to know. She would no doubt be witness to them again before he left. If he did, would she figure out the real reason for traveling a continent?

CHAPTER 8

*A*isling watched as the great hulk waivered. Dropping his shovel, Bastion grabbed his head with both hands falling to the ground.

"Bastion! Bastion, are you in trouble? Do I need to get help?" She shoved at this shoulder, but it didn't seem to have any impact on bringing him back to his senses, or for that matter budging him at the least.

She watched, leaving her hand on his shoulder to be a support in the only way she could, human touch. He sat rocking back and forth, holding his head. Having no idea what–

A flash of white seized Aisling propelling them somewhere else. *No longer in by the rubble, but Inside in a bedroom to be exact, with candles flickering casting gentle shadows throughout. Aisling looked around and saw Bastion.*

Oh My.

Bastion was kneeling on the bed, back turned, naked his strong thighs and backside flexing to hold his position with a strange birthmark on his right thigh of a triangle interweaved with a circle, before getting a better look at the mark, she noticed he wasn't just holding himself, but there were an extra set of arms and legs to the mix. Aisling's heart thumped a loud tattoo.

Who was this woman? If Aisling could get close enough and peak around... The woman looked up over Bastion's shoulder and trailed kisses from his neck down his well-muscled shoulder and arm, head lolling back once the woman finished eyes closed. It was her. She was her. Aisling was the woman in Bastion's arms.

How could this be possible? Hoping it would make sense. Heat flooded her body and, in that moment, she wasn't watching the scene play out, but Bastion actually held her in his arms. His gentle, reverent touch pulled emotions from Aisling that had been buried for months. In his arms she felt loved.

this wasn't real. A dream? Bastion was in some sort of a fit again and now she joined him. To pull herself out of such fanciful nonsense, Aisling took a step back releasing the grip on Bastion's shoulder, not realizing how strong it had been. In that instant reality threw her in the forest by the burned-out manor and Bastion still sat holding his head and shaking.

Air, clean and cool filled her lungs making her gasp. Aisling used a nearby tree to ease down onto the ground. How should one go about calming a stomach jumping and fluttering so? She managed to bring a hand up to her cheek to feel the heat there, but the hand in question chilled her, it even looked blue when Aisling pulled it up to face height to inspect it.

Bastion took in a great breath and gasped for more. Looking around wild eyed and setting his gaze on Aisling he made an obvious attempt to compose himself.

There were so many questions, but knew they were part of each other. Somehow. If what she saw was their future it would be interesting indeed.

Steeling her emotions to not giveaway what just happened,

Aisling crawled to him and reached out to set a hand on his shoulder but pulled back at the last moment. "Bastion, are you quiet, all right? You, you had a spell of some sort. Do you remember?"

He sat looking at her. Aisling feared what the blank stare might mean. She had heard of people having such spells and not having any recollection of it after, but could he lose days?

"Bastion?" she asked more quietly, not wanting to disturb him.

"What? Yes, yes I am fine."

"What? No, I don't think so." Aisling reached out and put a hand on his shoulder to stop him from getting up and putting this behind them without so much as an explanation. "You are not leaving until you tell me what is going on with you. First, I come upon you having some sort of a dream by the manor, now, you fall to the ground and go into a fit. If you are not well, I need to know Senor Guaire. I need to know what to do if this happens again."

He sat quiet for several moments, then sat back fully on the ground, stretching his long, large legs out in front of him. Aisling couldn't help imagine those large muscles roping down his long body, glistening in the sun rays as they danced through the openings in the trees. Heat rose and shot down into the belly and she had to mask a groan with a cough. Once a woman has seen such a specimen naked, how does one ever see him with clothes on again and not simply envision him naked again? If that truly is what he looks like naked, clothing is highly over rated, and perhaps a crime against all that is good in the world. She took in a breath and looked up in time to catch him watching. A mix of emotions that danced across his face. Confusion. Humor. Something she didn't quite understand, but her body tingled in reaction to it.

"It is rude to stare at a lady." She pointed out, when he wouldn't stop.

"Yes, I am sure it is." His only reply but kept looking.

"Listen, I do not want to pry into matters that are none of my business, but if you are ill, I feel obligated to help."

"I am not ill," He commented dryly, "I have visions."

He turned back with a look of a boy hoping to be picked for a game. She wasn't sure what to say, but she believed him. After not getting a response from her he pressed on.

"I have had visions since I was a boy."

"You can see the future?" She asked.

"Sometimes. Sometimes, like when I hold an artifact or a bone, I can see the past."

Understanding dawned. "That is why you have been so successful as an archeologist. You get clues from your visions about where to look to find answers." Excitement welled inside her.

"You are not questioning me? Mocking me?" Bastion asked with wonder in his voice.

"Why would I?"

"Because it is not every day that a grown man claims to have visions." Bastion answered with a warning look in his eyes.

"Why do you choose to be with the dead, when you could tell people their fortunes?" She asked.

"Well, because I am not a character in a side show, and because I don't always have visions when I touch things or people. Sometimes nothing happens, and I cannot control when it does."

"Have you had any visions about me?" She asked, commending the nonchalance in her voice. Bastion on the other hand, unable to hide anything. He blanched and raked his hand through his dark long hair.

"You have." She declared. "What kind of vision?" "This is not a parlor trick Miss Lightowler." He grumbled and rose.

"That is not fair Senor Guaire. You cannot simply admit to having visions about a lady and not share them." She spat as she scrambled to her feet, getting caught up in a billow of skirts.

"I didn't say I had visions of you." He began cleaning up again.

"You didn't say you didn't, and I am sorry to report if you didn't already know, but your face does not hide your thoughts very well I am afraid."

He grunted and continued working ignoring her.

"I saw what you saw," She said, standing straight waiting for an argument.

"You what? You saw? But how?" He turned and grabbed Aisling by the shoulders. The blush and the heat she knew blazed in her eyes from remembering the scene gave Bastion the answer.

"Do all your visions come true?" she asked in a quiet voice. Not yet certain what answer to hope for. She sensed him recoil and pull away slightly, but not break contact.

"I have never known one not to." he stated, and he looked hard at her.

Aisling looked back into his wanting to ask if he had seen them married but knew the answer didn't matter. It should, but it didn't.

She reached up pulling his face down into a kiss. She closed her eyes and gave herself to the moment, to him. Bastion held himself stiff as she continued to kiss him, hoping he wanted the same. If the vision was correct they would have to get passed his trepidation of the situation. sliding a hand behind him, under his coat. His back muscles were taut, and they jumped and vibrated at a feather light touch. That was all it took.

Bastion growled or groaned, perhaps a scintillating mix of the two which wretched a similar reaction from Aisling's body unable to pull it back. They stood devouring each other in the middle of the manor foundation. All thought of the world around them forgotten, until Bastion broke the kiss and pulled back, like he was pulling two magnets apart.

"How?"

"I touched your shoulder when you fell to the ground. I must have made contact with you and your vision went to me."

"What–" He started, but she stopped him not wanting the awkward question to hang in the air.

"It was you. You were naked." She said the last not able to look at him. "You were with someone. I stepped closer to see." looking up.

At that he rose a brow.

"What? It wasn't like I could turn and leave the room, I didn't know how I had gotten there." She said defensive, but he just chuckled and didn't say anymore.

"When I got closer I saw that it was me, then..." She trailed off, not sure how to say the last part without giving away how innocent she was.

"Yes?" he coaxed reaching down and entwining their fingers bringing them to his lips to put a warm kiss on her knuckles.

"After I saw, it actually became me. I was– I was in your arms. We were making love." Aisling's cheeks burned.

"What are your thoughts and considerations about that?" He asked, not relinquishing the connection in their clasped hands and never breaking eye contact.

What would be the correct thing to say or do? English girls were not taught the protocol in this such situation. Was he looking for permission for her ruin? To say they would need to wed? If Aisling did the first she would be a wanton woman. If she did the second and he didn't want to marry her– well she didn't want to think about that.

"My thoughts are that I never expected to have this consideration when I finished my tea and ham this morning." pausing to gain courage, "I think I will have to know all you know about these visions you have had, starting with the first one to truly understand our predicament."

"I would never act on my visions without your consent." He swore, but they knew that a falsehood. Yesterday in the parlor was not at all the chance encounter she had thought. He blushed to the hairline on his forehead showing their like thinking.

"I am sorry for yesterday. I have never been in a situation before not able to control my–myself. It will not happen again." He released her hand and backed away.

"No, I didn't mind. It was a bit shocking and unexpected. We had just been formally introduced just yesterday morning, but..." She trailed off before sounding too needy.

CHAPTER 9

Standing taught, every muscle in his body hardened and froze waiting for the answer. Bastion had decided it would be best not to share his gift with Aisling now everything was changed.

"I am sorry," she finally continued, "but I am at a loss for what you expect me to say. If I say I am looking forward to the culmination of your vision, I am a wanton, but if I say I am a gently bred lady and should be shocked and angered by what I saw I may be fighting my destiny."

Before he could reach up and take her into his arms again, a rustling in the woods cooled him. With no time for Aisling to flee, he turned abruptly putting her behind him.

"I say," Desmond Landry came into the clearing once again and stopped. "Aisl– Miss Lightowler, good morning." Landry said after hiding his surprise. "I was not aware Count Guaire that you were familiar with other families in the area."

"Ah, yes. I am here visiting the Lightowlers." Was all Bastion offered.

"I see, well in any case, I am hosting a card game and billiards at my home tonight. I hadn't thought of it while we were talking but thought you might enjoy meeting some of the other gentlemen in the area."

The Englishman was talking to Bastion, but noted Landry never took his eyes off Aisling. Something strong and feral rose in Bastion. He forced it down, needing to be objective in this matter, but that something wanted nothing more than to beat Landry into the ground at that moment.

"Miss Lightowler, does your father have any specific plans for me this evening?" Bastion turned and attempted to give her very little consideration at all, to divert any question of propriety.

"Well, no I believe you are free to do as you would like Senor Guaire." She answered, "But I was sent by Papa to fetch you. He hoped to have luncheon and discuss your travels."

"Yes, of course. Thank you." Bastion said and turned back to Landy. His body reacted to Aisling's departure before the ground crunched under her feet. The sunbeams were no longer as warm as they had been just minutes ago. "Well, Lord Landry, it seems that I am at your disposal for the evening. When should I arrive?"

"Splendid!" Landry answered, seeming genuinely satisfied, "We will start with drinks at 7:00, followed by cards and food."

Bastion reached out to shake his hand. "Thank you, I very much look forward to it." He assured Landry and the two men parted.

Bastion finished picking up his tools and turned the gig back toward Lightowlers. Once Aisling stepped away Bastion's lungs were able to work and get air pumping through his body and unseizing his brain. Controlling unwilling emotions had always been a source of pride for him but had Landry not come back would she have left with her virtue intact? Thankfully they would never know.

Everything about that woman drove him mad. Just the scent of that mass of hair sent tendrils of lust snaking through his body. Men dreamed of lips so plump. Almost over so and the color of garnacha grapes, like the ones grown on his very own vineyard. When kissing her, he imagined they tasted of the wine itself. Bastion could drink from them and never be quenched.

The women he chose were usually more robust in stature. Aisling was a wisp of a thing. Bastion remembered the stories his mother told of the Xanax. Fairies who protected the weak and foiled the evil in the world. Could Aisling be his own personal Xanax?

He passed the halfway point on the trail, unable to concentrate on anything but his need, and the object of it. Bastion had spent most of the previous night waxing on about Aisling's eyes. He would swear as they kissed her eyelashes were so long that they fluttered against his cheek bone. Just remembering the feel of it, made him hard. Since when could he consider himself a poet?

Tonight's diversion would be very well placed, because if left alone in that house, with her down the hall, it was not certain he would prolong the inevitable. The only saving grace would be that she shared a room with Deidra, who Bastion knew would not take kindly to the stranger residing at their home to invade their bedroom and kidnap her sister.

Bastion loosened his neckcloth and unbuttoned his jacket, hoping some cool woodland air would clear his mind before he entered the house, searched out Aisling, and found a nice quiet closet to ravage her.

~

At seven o'clock precisely, Bastion's carriage rumbled up the drive of Landry manor. Bastion had been able to sneak into the house and to his room without bumping into or ravaging Aisling. Perhaps, she could feel the feral waves wafting from his very soul in the forest and ran to hide. Smart girl he thought with a bitter taste in his mouth. A grown man should be better at controlling his impulses. She should not have to hide, if in fact she was.

When he reached his room, the journal Lightowler promised lay on the edge of the bed, and a tray of cold meats, hard cheese, and bread. No doubt Aisling ordered that. Bastion spent the afternoon reading, eating, and making what were necessary and marking some pages but would need more information before knowing if any of it would be helpful. the book carried no visions either.

Now on the doorstep of the other parties to this great catastrophe he hoped to garner some more information. However, being connected to the Lightowlers may not help to loosen tongues. Perhaps the bottle of Spanish wine he brought with him from his personal stash would help.

The butler invited him, and led him to a well-appointed room, where ten or more men sat throughout talking, drinking, and smoking sweet smelling cigarillos.

"The fourth Count of Lugar de Sueno." The butler announced his presence, bowed and left the room shutting the double doors behind him.

Bastion stood as his host rose from a chair to greet him

"Ah Senor Guaire. I was not sure you would attend. Good to see you. Come let us get you a drink."

"Thank you. I brought this for you." Bastion handed him the bottle of wine and Desmond took it an examined the label.

"I am not familiar with this label I am afraid." Desmond remarked.

"It is my private label. We own a vineyard on our estate in Spain. This is quite a nice summer wine. Made from Garnacha grapes. This is my favorite batch yet."

"Thank you very much. I look forward to sampling this."

said and handed it off to a footman, who had a silver salver with a glass of brandy for Bastion. "Thomas, put this in my study, in the back of the drink trolley, will you? I don't want anyone to get into it before I have had a chance." He slapped Bastion on the shoulder. "Now, for introductions." Landry said and led Bastion around the room to make formal introductions.

Bastion was pleased at how accepting they all seemed, it had been his experience that people could be more like Lord Lightowler when meeting a stranger. Tight lipped and suspicious would not help his cause. Desmond settled back in his chair and offered Bastion the one next to him.

"I am sorry William, I missed the end of your recount of the horse race in Bath." Desmond said getting settled and the other men in the group waited. "If you please." motioning for William to retell his story,

"Oh sorry, do you partake in horse racing in Spain Count Sueno?"

"My brother was very much into anything concerning horses. We currently have a stable primarily filled with Andalusians." Bastion answered, only partially knowledgeable having spent time with the head groom and breeder only weeks before leaving.

"I have heard of those. Large, but very agile if I remember

correctly." Responded Lord Tardiff. A plump fellow with a shock of red hair, and cheeks almost the same color.

"Ah, yes. My brother and his head breeder were working on adding more Arabian blood into our stable to try and create a more slender, quicker version."

"Is it working do you think?" asked someone else to Tardiff's left. Bastion thought to remember his name Mr. Standthrope. That was it.

"I believe the breeder has been happy thus far. To be honest, until my brother's death I traveled extensively and therefore not familiar with the work my brother did with the horses in our stables. I can say that I have taken one of the recent off spring as my own mount and setting aside the fact that the beast is a stubborn one and prone to taking off on a gallop without warning he is very acceptable."

All the men laughed, nodded, and commented amongst themselves about the exuberance of young horses.

"William, again I have stopped you, please continue." Desmond finally prodded his friend.

"Oh, well nothing really too fantastical. I put a month's savings on Percival who was not the top pick for the race, but when I met him he just had that look about him, and he won. So, my point was that considering the lineage in the top three horses of that race, Percival should not have come into the top four. Sometimes it is more about the determination in the horse than the breeding."

Many of the men scoffed and grumbled at that ascertain. Bastion noted to himself to take the horse breeding more seriously when back in Spain, apparently there was something to all this.

"What has brought you across the continent to our small corner of the world?" Tardiff asked to change the subject.

"I am visiting Lord Lightowler and his family." Bastion answered

"How is old Lightowler? Haven't seen him out in society since–" Tardif began

"Since the discovery of the rose bush." Desmond finished for his friend and all the men in earshot laughed.

"Lord Lightowler is very much devoted to his study." Bastion agreed.

"It appeared that Aisling had been put in charge of you. I am not sure if I should congratulate you on your luck or pity you that you will never have a moments peace." Desmond commented dryly, and the other men chuckled.

"Better than Constance, you might very well find yourself encased in a lump of clay." Another jested and they all laughed.

"Aisling is a good duck just a bit too... ah, intense for my comfort. Once that woman gets an idea there is no reasoning. She will go to ground with it and remain until it has been exhausted."

"Are you close with Aisling?" Bastion asked, not rather interested in an answer if it is yes.

"You could say that. There was a time when I might have been persuaded to ask for her hand, but then came the issue with–" Desmond glanced over at Bastion and changed tact. Damn. "We seemed to grow apart, and I realized I needed a wife who would be more easily brought to tow, which does not describe any of the Lightowler girls, so I moved on."

"Lord Desmond, I am to tell you that the card room is ready. Food will be served once everyone is settled." The butler stopped the conversation in its track.

"Thank you, Felix." Desmond said.

"Well it is about time, Desmond, I was beginning to think the promise of food and cards but a ploy to get us to come and drink with you." Standthrope barked as the men rose and headed to the adjacent room. Many of the other men laughed and agreed. Bastion let the men go ahead as they all appeared to know where they were going.

Standthrope hung back as well and proffered a hand for the shaking. "Andrew Standthrope."

"Mr. Standthrope."

"Please call me Andrew."

"Very well, I am Bastion. I prefer that actually, still not used to the title. It is not so far removed from being my brother's." Bastion admitted.

"Sorry to hear. I am the third son of a clerk. Desmond allows me to join in, he thinks it makes for a more diverse entertainment than just those of high rank. Bastion and Andrew strode into the card room and both took seats at a table together. Desmond was at a table across the room, so there would be no more questioning him for the time being.

"Please don't think me rude, but might I enquire as to how Miss Deidra is fairing these days?"

Bastion looked at Andrew, and he could see the stark interest and concern span his features.

"Since her mother is away visiting a relative, she has been very busy since I arrived, but she appears to be doing well, but I have only just met her, so my impressions are very singular."

Two more men settled themselves at their table already deep in their own conversation.

Andrew nodded and said nothing Letting this information sink in.

"I have not called, I should, but have not." Andrew continued as the other men continued a conversation they had been involved in. "She wrote me a few times, but I have not taken the time to respond, and it has been some time since she has penned me anything." He admitted, with a pained look on his face.

Bastion wasn't sure what to say. He got the impression a portion of the him wanted Bastion to tell him that Deidra was a watering can of tears, pining. The other half however, seemed happy that his callous behavior hadn't had any ill effects. "Did you have a row?" Bastion asked coaxing him into talking about the scandal.

"No, no nothing like that." Andrew jumped to defend. "We just– well there is–"

"The scandal?" Bastion asked taking pity on him in the hopes of speeding up his recount.

Andrew shifted in his seat and looked up at the other two men who were deep into their own conversation waiting for everyone to be settled and begin play.

"Well, yes." Andrew admitted sheepishly, "I–I have no idea what to think. My mother is beyond herself at the possibility that there is a murdering family among us."

Bastion wasn't as familiar with the Lightowlers as their neighbors, but he was certain they were not a family of murderers carrying on a family legacy, "Do you believe they could all be a family of murderers?" Bastion asked as seriously as possible without breaking a smile at the absurdity of it.

"No." Andrew said very quickly in the Lightowlers' defense, "but it would send my mother into histrionics if I were to continue pursuing Deidra, ah, Miss Deidra in light of the accusations." He would not look Bastion in the eye.

"If I could but think of a way to help them sort this farce out." Bastion commented, hoping to gain an ally in the young, love struck Andrew.

At the news of someone wanting to help and not just perpetuate a rumor Standthrope perked up.

"Do you think it possible? To help them I mean? Is it not already too late?"

"Gentlemen. Are we going to play cards or just sit and talk like my mother's luncheon ladies?" Desmond broke into the chatter. "We are playing Faro. The buy in is 10 pounds. Felix will be around to collect. Count Guaire, are you familiar with Faro?" Desmond spoke across the room.

"I am Lord Landry. I was very successful at keeping my brother's pockets lighter than my own because of it." Bastion assured him and gained himself a round of laughter from the others.

Felix came to their table with a fresh deck of cards handing them to one of the other men at the table. "Well, I guess that makes me the dealer," he said breaking open the deck and shuffling. "I'm Egton, this is Mr. Cook." He introduced themselves and began play. There was no time after that for Andrew and him to discuss anything but the cards.

On a break well on toward midnight, Bastion found Andrew at the refreshment table, after being separated and put at different tables as men fell out of favor with their prospect gambling Gods. Bastion was happy with his own winnings thus far as well.

"Were you serious earlier? About helping the Lightowlers?" Andrew asked straight away.

"Why yes. Wouldn't you think it more prudent to help them than sit back and become part of the problem?" Bastion's comment bordered cruel, but really holding a whole family accountable and questioning their own respectability based solely on a story that no one can agree on from almost one hundred years ago? His own mother spoke of how her family over the years had to flee or move when rumors of their ancestors would come on the wind. What those rumors were, his mother would never speak of and tell the children that it was so long ago and they were so far from where they originated that it would no longer follow them.

"I would. Very much so. How can I help?" Andrew asked with all the enthusiasm of a man in love. Perhaps if Bastion was not able to successfully clear their ancestor there might be a way to set the rumors and nonsense about their current respectability to rest. That would be one sort of a win. He did not want Aisling to have difficulties throughout her life, once he went back to Spain.

"What can you tell me of the incident in question?" Bastion asked.

"I only know what has been said, as most of us were not alive, and those that were would have been children and infants." Andrew admitted wryly.

"I do know someone alive that might have a good recollection of the events, but I am not sure how reliable she would be." Andrew offered, as he took another crust of bread and slice of ham into his mouth.

"Who?" Bastion asked with interest, "and how old is she?"

"And that is the rub. I am not sure anything she tells us will make sense, or even be accurate. Her days and even years seem a jumble at times." Andrew admitted. "The woman lived with The Landry's. Her mother a maid and father a groom. I believe she was eight or nine years of age Which means any memories will be influenced by a child's imagination."

Bastion was not about to share with his new ally. "Any information could leads us to something. Can you arrange a meeting?"

"Yes, of course. She is retired now, but my mother visits during her charity visits each week. I will go straight away in the morning. Should I send word to the Lightowler estate?"

"Yes, that will be best."

"Well, it looks as though we have settled our final table and you gentlemen have gained a seat each." Desmond came up to the two and slapped them both on the back. "I have to say Andrew, I was surprised to see you tonight. How many times have I extended an invitation in the past few months?"

"Yes, you have been very generous with your invitations. I have been out of town, and very busy, but I am here now."

"Yes, yes you are, and I am looking forward to helping relieve you of some of those funds you hold so dear." Desmond said with a bark of laughter.

"Well, you are welcome to make the attempt, but I fear the one we all should fear is Count Guaire. He is currently in possession of a good amount of my funds already."

Bastion chuckled, but perhaps he should not divest his host and his new acquaintance of all their winnings. Perhaps humble himself for the greater good.

"Shall we gentlemen?" Bastion said grabbing a green apple from the table and taking a large bite as the men crossed the room. If he tried hard enough, perhaps he would stop thinking about Aisling. He highly doubted it though.

CHAPTER 10

The front door creaked in silent protest when Bastion returned to the Lightowler home at almost half passed one in the morning. Trying not to wake anyone, since he was certain a house with a horticulturist specializing in roses and filled with young yet to be married daughters was not a household that made Its staff wait up late for the family to return from routes and social parties.

Just as he suspected the main hall vacant of light, with only a single unlit candle sitting on the table by the stairs leading to the bed chambers. A match sitting beside it. At least someone considered his comfort. Aisling.

The candle spit and sputtered until settling down to a yellow glow to light his way.

Bastion made his way up the stairs and along the deep hallway toward his room. Passing Aisling's door his steps slowed. He wanted to wake her and tell her they had help and perhaps answers, but more than that he just wanted to see her.

Would that mass of dark curls be hanging unbound down her back? What does she look like roused from sleep? He could imagine dark eyes framed by heavy, thick lashed lids, and rosy cheeks from the warmth of the covers. Bastion bet she would make little mewling sounds when coaxed awake with his kisses.

Biting back a curse while tamping down an overwhelming urge to enter the room and take her captive in his own, forced himself to continue to his own room. The purpose of coming to England and meeting Aisling was to lessen his desire, but to the contrary, he wanted her more than breath. Perhaps once his vision played out it would tamper his desire and be too late for them both. Closing his door on a sigh hoping to shut out his lascivious thoughts, noting the connecting doors to his nephew's room had been closed so not to wake him or Perez. He undid his cravat and draped it over a chair. Next Bastion set to ridding himself of his boots and overcoat.

Once settled in a chair Bastion laid his head back against the cushioned back and closed his eyes. He dealt in bones and artifacts, not living fallible people. This situation plunged him into unfamiliar waters. In no version of his life would he be considered a detective, it was a hell of a muddle. Her image danced behind his eyes. A woman who had a difficult time believing there were people in the world who wished ill for other people.

A soft knock on his door, brought him out of the chair like a gun had been shot in the hallway. He was not lucky enough to have Pilchard ignore his edict of not waiting up to assist him. Every muscle in his body went rigid as every nerve came alive, sending shivers throughout. Aisling. Please Lord, let her not be in her night dress and barefoot.

Another soft knock, accompanied with an even softer, "Bastion? Bastion are you there?"

For whatever sin he committed, these next ten minutes would either absolve him or send him straight to hell.

Bastion went to the door and cracked it so that light from his one single candle washed over Aisling's form illuminating a heart shaped face. He inwardly groaned, seeing that she did in fact still wear a stark white nightdress.

"May I come in?" She asked

"I am not sure–"

"It is cool out here and if we are to talk about what you found out, we cannot do that best with a door between us." She insisted laying her hand on the door pushing it wider and breezing past him before he could protest and protest he should. He was certain more conversation would be productive with a door, wall, battlements, and a cage between them right now.

"I am sure Miss Lightowler that any news I may have will not change the tide of your predicament before morning. We can discuss all I found out at the breakfast table."

"Nonsense, it is always best to discuss things while they are fresh in one's mind." Aisling continued with no understanding of the muddle she was making of his mind.

"Miss Lightowler–"

"Aisling. We, I believe are well past the point of Miss and Senor. Don't you quite agree?"

Oh yes, yes, he agreed. They should be to the point of inaudible noises and unintelligible speech.

"Aisling, you should not be here." He said, trying to sound firm. All the while stalking toward her, with an overwhelming urge to possess. "It is not a good idea that you are here." He warned again, with a gravelly voice hinting at barely tethered manners. their closeness required Aisling to shift looking up at his face. His hands reached out drawing her closer to him. He noted she did not pause but came easily into his arms. "Aisling." Bastion bit out, sounding pained to his own ears.

His mouth took hers, when she opened it slightly to lick those luscious lips in a nervous behavior. He groaned at the sweet, warm taste and the way her body gave into him in the way Aisling's body was taut with anticipation but yielding to come into closer contact with his own body, that at the moment was humming so loud it might well wake the servants.

He pulled back almost panting and cupped her cheek with his hand. Aisling was as warm and soft as she looked, his calloused hand slid over the satin skin. A groan escaped him when she bent resting in his palm, when she turned her head and kissed him on the fleshy part by his thumb it almost undid him pulling away as if burned.

The cotton of the serviceable night dress prickled like thistle weed all over her body standing in the dark room. The weight of Bastion's scrutiny like an anvil. She shouldn't be in his room. He was correct. By sounding his warning, he proved his gentlemanly side. The only trouble with that, she didn't care to be warned.

Aisling would consider herself a very logical, pragmatic girl. Never making rash decisions and always weighing the pros and cons of every situation. Out of all her sisters she was the one to be left home because she didn't think it prudent to go out, for various reasons.

She would be the one to remain and care for father if their mother chose not to return. Didn't she deserve a monocom of happiness, even for a brief time? Deidra agreed. After talking at length with Deidra for some time after the kiss, they were in agreement, that based on their current predicament, and the makeup of all the sisters, Aisling was the most likely to choose spinsterhood to care for their father, over the others, so there would be no husband to take up issue if Aisling chose to take a lover before marriage. If there wasn't going to be a marriage, could it be considered improper?

Aisling new the answer to that question, which sent a new wave of anticipation through her body and warmed those parts that had cooled the instant Bastion stepped away.

"Bastion." Was all she said to his protests. A quiet plea.

Cool night air seeped through the cotton as he took another step back, obviously fighting the urge to–well to either flee or gobble her up whole, she couldn't be sure. She took a step closer.

"You showed me it is our destiny." She said, reaching up to touch his whiskered cheek. For only a moment he leaned in and closed his eyes. "What about after?" in a low, gruff voice that sent tingles to the pit of her stomach. Everything he said and did caused an immediate physical response.

"I–I don't know. You did not have that in the vision." She explained, hoping her voice did not waiver as much as it sounded.

"That is my point." He said, turning from her and walking to the window on the other side of the large four poster bed. "I have not seen what happens after either. I cannot promise you will not be hurt and I could not live with myself if I hurt you."

"Then don't." Aisling suggested. It made perfect sense. If he didn't want to hurt, her just choose not to. "I will not expect marriage of you Bastion, if that is your fear. Deidra and I have talked at length and it makes perfect sense for me to choose a lover, as I will be the one to not marry and care for my father, if mother does not return."

He growled low in his throat, and even without the added benefit of seeing his face, she knew the dangerous intent she would see on his face if she could. She took a step back for good measure.

"What do you mean you will not marry? Isn't that what women of your station do in England? Is it so much different here than in Spain?"

"Well, yes most women do, but in certain circumstances, like my family's, it only makes sense that I remain with father–"

"Why? Why you?" He asked finally turning and advancing on until his stockinged toes touched her bare ones. She suppressed a squeal.

"Well, well because I–" Pausing, Aisling tried to formulate what didn't need to be said between two sisters, "It is just so and difficult to explain." She turned from him, not wanting him to see the emotion plain on her face. She had always wanted to marry, and have a family, but Papa took more to her than the others and Aisling could persuade him in ways the other girls could not.

"No. It is an excuse."

With that challenge in the air, she swung on him finger wagging in the air. "I beg your pardon? You have little to no knowledge of me past my letters and how my lips taste." She bit out. "I do not think you have leave to comment on my life choice."

One moment Bastion was set apart the next he in her space glowering. "My dear, when you and your sister have tagged me as the poor sod to make you wholly ineligible to marry, I do think it affords me some intimacy's in our conversation I wouldn't otherwise be allowed."

Having no argument for his reasoning, Aisling eyed him hard. If she was hoping for a specific man to take her innocence that did give said man leave to speak freely of things he did not belong to she decided. "You are of course welcome to say what you will, but it does not mean that I must be inclined to take your suggestions."

She stepped up to him placed her hand on his arm. "I understand your concern Bastion, but I have considered this for some time. Deidra and I have spoken of it often since my mother has left. The two of us are left to keep the household running and considering what will happen to us all. I had resigned myself months ago to not having my own home and family, but I had not considered what else I would be giving up. You made me realize that aspect which an innocent would not first think on."

"I am sorry." Bastion apologized as his jaw seemed to tighten and clench in the flickering candle light. "Had I known it would set you on this path, I would not have reacted as I did." He said, his eyes softening and his jaw loosening a bit.

"I am not." She answered, as he bent and took her mouth with his. A kiss this time gentle and undemanding. Melting into his embrace he moved from her lips to trail feather light kisses from the corner of her mouth along her jaw to her earlobe. Continuing down to the hollow where the collarbone met her throat. Tendrils of desire spread and licked at the flame forming in her belly. She wanted him not certain what that all entailed, but right now more of his wicked tongue was fine.

Aisling's night dress must have come untied, because before she knew it, Bastion's mouth traced the edge of her shoulder. The cool air of the room mixed with his ministrations tightened the now exposed nipple. She sucked in a breath as it puckered and tightened, rubbing against his hand-embroidered waistcoat sending shock waves to her toes with every rub.

Aisling had had been unaware about the sensations one's body could experience and thought she might expire, until Bastion looked at her in the candlelight, with heavy lidded eyes and flushed cheeks. His smile one of mischief and trouble and promise. Aisling was unsure until he bent his head to her breast.

CHAPTER 11

"Oh my." She moaned and gasped as his hot mouth encircled her nipple. Waves of sensations rocked her body and she had to grasp his arms to stay upright. "Bastion." She whispered his name, feeling her heart tighten at the sound.

Bastion groaned, sending vibrations to the furthest reaches of her body. "Meu." He professed taking his mouth away only to slide the nightdress off the other shoulder to give that bared breast the same attention as he did wicked things with the abandoned nipple slipping it and rolling it between his fingers. "Mine." He said in English to no one continuing his onslaught of sensation.

"God Bastion." Aisling's legs went weak and would have slumped to the ground had he not been there to scoop her up and find a bed. The same bed in the vision. The bed that she watched as he– as he– heat filled her at the thought of what she had witnessed. Settling between her legs in an odd sensation.

"Aisling." He panted placing her on the bed on her knees, staring down with hungry eyes. "Aisling, you are a treasure, but

I fear this is something you will regret. I could not bear being your regret." He whispered Leaning his forehead on hers. His breathing labored, and she could see how taut his muscles were under the cover of his waistcoat and shirt.

She reached up with shaking hands and began with the top button of his waistcoat reveling in how snug the fabric fit over his muscled chest. He groaned unmoving. Aisling knew it would not matter what assurances she gave, Bastion was a gentleman and would argue against any argument for. It would be easier to show him. Once divested of his ornately decorated waistcoat, he willingly pulled his shirt over his head to reveal the most sculpted body Aisling had ever seen. A lady did not have opportunity to see many shirtless men, but those she had spied in the fields paled when put up against Bastion Guaire. Constance would swoon at how perfectly sculpted he was. She set a shaking hand on his chest over his heart and it beat a healthy tattoo on her palm. This was real, it wasn't just a vision. His chest and torso shimmered in the candle light. Every place she touched his muscles would twitch and roll in response. Bastion's stark face gave away nothing.

"Am I hurting you?" She asked about to pull her hand back. Without opening his eyes, he trapped the hand and pressed it into his side where it had laid.

"No, not hurting. I am just trying to let you explore, but all I want is to divest you of that Godawful night dress and bring you to your pleasure."

The thought went straight to her head. Not at all certain what he meant, but her body reacted in such a way she would not refuse for any reason. Sliding a hand down his side, it glided over a ribbon like muscle that went from his hip below the waistband of his pants. Aisling didn't know its name, but so far it was her favorite. Fingering along the ridge of it and dipping a finger under the waistband to continue following its decent. Bastion made a noise deep in his throat and grabbed her hand to stop it. "It is a game, meu amor until you venture there. That is when it may not be undone." His expression hard lines and tight muscled jaw. Aisling knew if she wanted to stop he would. This man, the one she barely knew and only really understood via his papers and essays, and letters. She trusted him implicitly.

With the coyest of smiles she took up his hand brought it to her lips, placing a kiss in the center of his palm. He closed his eyes. He did not however, try protest when, with the finger still just below his waistband, she continued sliding down following that muscle until her finger stopped, nestled a patch of coarse hair. Her free hand started at his tight forearm and slid over to his chest caressing each bend and curve until it reached the button of his pants.

Bastion reached down and flicked the button loose. A fine trail of hair sent her eyes from his belly button down to below the placard of his breeches. In one fluid motion she almost missed, he shoved the pants passed his hips to bunch on the floor at his feet. Bastion whirled around sitting on the bed to divest his calves and feet of the tightfitting stockings and just like that he was naked.

Aisling's breath caught, and the room dimmed. He stood again and turned. Aisling, still kneeling on the bed watched how his muscles ebbed and flowed with his movements. Her hands itched to be on him again, this time exploring with no barriers. Before she could reach for him, his hands reached out sliding the billowing nightgown down passed her hips, bared to the world. The innocent in her reached up to cover.

"Stop." Bastion commanded. "You are more beautiful than in my visions. Fermoso. So, beautiful." He said with a reverence that made Aisling's throat catch. She had been kissed and courted, but no one had ever reacted to her in such a manner. She could feel the emotion come off him in waves.

Before Aisling lost her nerve, she reached out to touch his chest and with slow metered movements trailed down his body to the nest of hair. Tentative and uncertain how to proceed.

Aisling's body instinctively knew things, she gave in and followed the time worn instinct within. With eyes closed her hand wrapped around him forcing a groan, "Aisling" half plea half warning it bolstered her bravado.

Where other parts of his body were smooth and taut his penis was like satin but at the same time hard. She slid her hand along the length enjoying the feel.

"Aisling, you might just kill me." Bastion ground out as he moved to the side, breaking the contact between them and lifting himself on the bed. She almost lost her balance as the well sprung mattress gave under the weight of his body.

Bastion came up behind her and wrapped his arms around her body, taking each breast in his hands and kissing the back of her neck. The feel of his lightly hairy, bare chest against her back was— well it simply the best feeling ever. His strength created a protective cocoon from the world, and if she were going to open herself up to fits of fancy would say his love. But, Aisling was nothing if not pragmatic. She knew Bastion would make this enjoyable but made sure to have no illusions that love would ever be part of their attachment.

Instead of dwelling on that which might not be, she leaned back into his chest, opening to his wandering hands and reveled in the feel. Every sensation would be catalogued, every emotion, for a time she needed it more.

"Aisling," he whispered, "You are amazing." Bastion trailed his hand across her stomach and lower until his entire hand stilled on the mound of dark curls. Unbidden, she froze. He waited, for Aisling to become accustomed to the feel of another person having access to such a private area. Once every muscle relaxed and she sunk more deeply into his broad chest, he brushed the curls from the opening and slid his finger between the folds.

The intrusion pointed every sensation to that one point. Her belly tightened and jumped, and her thighs tingled. With a gentleness that belayed his size and strength, he slid one finger inside. Her hips rose to meet his hand and so started a slow rhythm she never knew she knew. After several minutes of such ministrations, he bent and kissed behind her ear. "You are ready meu amor. Lie down love."

Bastion slid from behind her, and went the wardrobe bending low to pull a carriage blanket from the bottom. One she saw the footmen bring in from his coach when they brought his things. "I am not certain there will be blood, but as your first time, it is not untypical. As the only man in a house of women, I am certain a maid would have concerns when she came to change the sheets. This will be less awkward for us all." He explained climbing back on the bed, and slid the blanket spread out underneath her making sure that no white sheets or blankets were draped over.

"Don't be frightened. I will do my best to make the discomfort as small as possible." He said reassuringly and walked his arms alongside her body rubbing his against her all the way to capture a kiss. until she was dizzy.

The weight of him settling between her legs decadent. Aisling's hips rose, and she began rubbing against him. Bastion made a sound deep in his chest more feral than proper gentleman, and rose up positioning himself, in one motion slid home and captured the cry in his mouth.

The pinch surprised her forcing a cry, but with his mouth over hers swallowing it as soon as it was free. Tears sprang to her eyes and she sucked in several deep breaths. To his credit Bastion stopped moving to allow Aisling a chance to acclimate to the new feeling and brushed a tear from the corner of each of her eyes.

"Do you wish me stop?" He asked, waiting for an answer, but Aisling was not sure how to answer. If that pain would continue when he moved again she did want him to stop, but she had read enough to know that it couldn't feel like all the time, or women would not be interested in taking husbands and lovers to bed. "Aisling, darling, I would love to give you an eternity to decide your next move, but if you don't make your choice soon, I will be lost. If you want me to stop, I will do it now, but you need to say so." He sounded almost in pain and very impatient if not. She looked in his eyes and saw the barely reined in desire fighting his control.

"Don't. Stop." She managed and wound her legs around his narrow hips and pulled him down for another kiss. Bastion pulled her to him with one arm and held tight keeping as much contact as possible. The rhythmic motion no longer pinched so to Aisling's relief. After a fashion need spiraled. One she couldn't have explained with words because she didn't understand it herself, Need spiraled through Aisling's body with every stroke. "Bastion, oh, Bastion."

"Let go my love, just let it take you." pressing harder into her, touching everywhere at once with his hands. She reached up and caught the leather strap that held his too long hair back and it washed over his shoulders blanketing them both from the world. He reached down with his hand and touched– It didn't matter where. She was falling and soaring at once. "Oh–" Overwhelmed by feeling, sensation, and emotion all at once.

"Aisling!" Bastion growled before pushing one more time and stopping deep, burying his face in her neck until his release finished. He fell to the side, but only enough to not crush her. They lay in silence only the sound of their breaths mingling in the darkness. The candle having long since burned itself out.

"Are you all right?" He asked, after a while, brushing hair from her cheek.

"I– I am not certain how I feel." She answered honestly. "I do not think I will ever feel the way I did yesterday." He chuckled softly and rubbed her bare belly with his finger. "I hope that is a good thing." He commented.

"I– yes." She said and sat up right with renewed energy, "Can we do it again?" She asked with more enthusiasm.

Bastion rose and paced to the window, pulling back the heavy curtain letting the moon light spill into the room. Aisling watched him pad to the water basin and draw a bowl from the pitcher grabbing a piece of linen before returning to the bed with both. He began wiping her down. Washing away any signs of their love making. "I think you will be sore enough in the morning, that you will be happy that we stop now." Unable to argue with his reasoning as she had never experienced the day after love making before. "Will it hurt like that every time?" She asked.

"No, the next time it shouldn't hurt at all, and you may be sore after a night of love making, but it will be a good sore." He assured her. A pang of something close to jealousy filled her at the thought of him having this knowledge from other women he had bedded. How many had there been and were all virgins? She did have the good sense not to voice her questions knowing that would surely spoil the moment, so she bit them back and tried to force a smile and concentrate on now. She would miss him, more than should be allowable when he went back to Spain, but that would not be now.

Once finished cleaning the area, unaware of Aisling's inner struggle he climbed back into bed, reached down pulling up the covers around them. Bastion pulled her into the circle of his arms and body. His own long hair spilled over their shoulders tickling her nose with the smell of cedar soap and the out of doors. Holding tight enough to show he wanted her, at least for now. Aisling let her eyes close and body go slack. She would steal herself against the future in the morning, for now she just wanted the be the woman in Bastion's arms.

CHAPTER 12

The smell of moss and dirt filled his nostrils as he strode through the woods. It was dusk, and a fog rolled in, licking at his boots as he trudged along. Why back in the woods? Bastion wondered to himself but kept walking with determined steps. A screech filled the silent calm of the woods and sent chills down his spine. Bastion ran toward the scream. A woman's scream. Breaking through the tree line he came to an abrupt stop in the open. There in front of him a familiar scene. Three people tied at the stake as the flames swirled around them. A mob of angry people stood not helping, but in fact cheering.

"Bastion," he heard his name, but knew no one around him. Glancing again at the three burning. One of the women looked directly at him, calling to him. She knew him. He took a step forward and she broke eye contact. When he looked more closely, the woman's dark hair hung over her face, but the slight form covered by an over-sized white dress sent a chill through him.

Bastion ran through the crowd to see better. He hoped upon hope it was not Aisling, but something told him—

"Bastion, this is your legacy." the words playing in his head. When he split the crowd and came to the safety of the circle of people just outside the rings of fire, the woman looked up again. The sight filling him with relief and pain in one breath. The woman on the pyre was not Aisling, but those eyes. This stranger's eyes and mouth were unmistakably his mother's and his brother's. This woman was a relative. The other two people burning looked his way and they too were unmistakable in their features. These people were relatives to him. He had to rescue them, save them. The flames were too hot.

"You're the legacy" he heard the woman saying, but she was not speaking just staring at him. "You are our legacy." He he–

Bastion came awake with a start. The room still dark and curled up next to him Aisling slept on. No mob and no burning pyres consuming relatives he had never met.

Rolling onto his back flinging his free arm over his eyes to block out the room. Why? This horrific scene had meaning to him, but what? It must be a vision of the past, but it felt different. His visions came from objects, this came from him. Next to him, Aisling shifted and made a little mewling sound in her sleep. Bastion uncovered his eyes and turned to study this woman—his woman.

"Damn." He whispered to himself. What a fool's errand. Having a vision did not justify being an ass. He was a man, who in his estimation had experienced love making enough times to better control his urges than this and using a vision as an excuse beyond intolerable

Bastion reached out and took a lock of hair lounging on the pillow and twirled it around his finger reveling at the silky smoothness of it. It smelled of rose water and lemon. He smiled to himself at that. The daughter of a man who studies roses should indeed smell of them. Placing a soft kiss in the riot of curls on his pillow, Bastion breathed in deeply her smell.

"What am I to do with you now?" A sleeping Aisling did not answer. She needed to be roused, without Bastion being pulled back into the spell to get her back before the servants woke or worse, his nephew, who upon waking insisted on coming in to jump on his bed and make certain he woke with the sun. The rest would untangle itself in time. "Aisling," rubbing her bare arm. She mumbled something curling into a tighter ball under the covers. She looked so young, so full of life. So, unlike the worried young woman trying to rescue an entire family legacy, while sacrificing her happiness to the cause. "My sweet, it is time to rouse. We must get you back."

Aisling stretched out lifting her arms, which in turn pulled the blankets down exposing two rosy, peaked nipples atop perfectly delectable mounds. Bastion's hands itched to replace the covers. She opened her eyes looking around with a moment of bewilderment. A look of confusion and fear passed, and Bastion spoke quickly to assure her.

"Aisling, you are in my room. Do you remember last night?" Bastion asked. The red that colored her from neck to hairline told him the memory was returning. She turned and looked at him with sleep filled eyes. Eyes that were almost as enticing as her pleasure filled eyes from last night. Every muscle wanted nothing more than to kiss the sleep from them and work up the pleasure again.

Just as Bastion wanted to fling himself from the bed and into the coolness of the morning air, she reached out and laid a hand on his chest and leaned in toward him. He reached out and grasp her hand in his own and as gently and kindly as he could removed it from his skin. Her touch burned and did not help his situation.

"Darling, there is nothing in the world I would like more than to repeat our experience from last night, but it is close to morning, closer than it should be. We have to get you back to your room before we are found out."

At the mention of being caught the sleep fell from her eyes and she went to throw back the covers and realized she was naked. Aisling pulled the covers back into herself. Bastion chuckled and reached over the side of the bed picking up the forgotten night dress that had spent the night on the floor. Watching it get wretched over her head covering all that milky white, soft skin he decided when she was truly his, all her nightdresses would be shredded.

As she continued to wrestle with the billowing fabric, Bastion rose from his bed and sauntered across the floor to pick up his trousers and slip them on. He smiled to himself, because the moment he exposed himself all sound on the bed ceased. her gaze heated him. Bastion knew women liked the way he was built and using that knowledge to his advantage another skill.

She made an attempt to change the subject. "We never did discuss–" Bastion cut her off.

"You need to be quiet, if my nephew wakes his first task every morning is to come in and wake me. I don't think we want that yet."

"I–oh I suppose we do not." She said quietly and remained silent dressing and tying her hair back in some kind of knot that did not require pins. She looked at the clock on the mantle. "I should be fine getting back to my room alone. No one rises until six o'clock and some of the servants are not about until later. I will not meet anyone who would question me." She was busy not making eye contact.

Bastion refused to let her leave without remembering what passed and the passion that they could have again. If he was already going to hell might as well put in for an extended stay.

He stepped in front of her when she stepped toward the door and wound his arms around her waist. "Aisling. Aisling look at me love." He said quietly, raising her chin with the side of his pointer finger. "Why won't you look at me? Was last night so horrible?"

"What?" she looked surprised at his train of thought, "No," she said quickly, "No, it quite pleasant." She amended with what Bastion assumed she considered an even tone. He could hear the husky undertone that gave away her reaction.

"Good," he pulled Aisling closer to him, and let his arousal prove his interest. "I found it very pleasurable. I found you very pleasurable, Aisling." He dropped his head and touched warm lips with his. Hot sweet air rushed out of her lungs on a sigh as she fell into him and gave herself up to the pleasure of the kiss.

He had no intentions of dragging her back into his bed now but did want to keep the wave of pleasure on the surface until their next encounter. He pulled back after several minutes of plundering her mouth. Sweeping a clump of hair away. "I shall see you at breakfast Aisling." And with that, he opened the door and sent his future out into the world a true woman, when the last time she walked down her father's hallway she was but a girl.

Aisling crept down the hallway with only the moonlight to light her way. She might be able to dismiss it as dream, if she didn't feel soreness in places an innocent should not. A small smile spread across her face, tightening her cheeks. Her lips hung plump and heavy, if she looked in the mirror they would be swollen and pink, like they were after their first kiss in the parlor.

It was a firm conviction. Marriage would not be expected. It would not be fair. If she hadn't touched his shoulder she would not have known of the vision and therefore, would not have taken advantage of the situation. Now the question would be how to not live out a life alone with a broken heart.

Padding softly into the room shared by her closest sister, Deidra roused only a moment before falling back to sleep. Which was for the best. Aisling did not want to be hounded with so many questions. She dragged her favorite reading chair over the carpet in silence and positioned it in front of the window, where she sat down, bare feet on the window sill. The moon hung low in the sky and before long the first tender rays of morning would lighten the whole world. Aisling wrapped her arms around her knees and laid her head atop them and tried to reason out what had just happened between them.

Would there be an opportunity for them to do that again? Did she want to do that again? Did he want to do that again? They could not be promised the opportunity would arise again, but on the other questions swirling in an already frayed mind, Aisling could say; Yes. Now keenly aware of what spinsters gave up she would never allow any woman she cared for to give that up.

Her concern now, becoming emotionally affected by the intimate contact. Unprepared for the onslaught of emotion to being held and touched in such a way to bring pleasure she understood now how a young miss could mistake ardent love with a man's lustful behavior. A shiver sizzled down her spine and settled low in her belly. She moaned inwardly, hoping to gain some control before meeting him at the breakfast table in a few hours.

She could call for a tray, but that would put an extra unnecessary burden on the staff and prove her a coward. Now, to the question about if he wanted to do it again, after that sendoff kiss this morning, she would have to say that yes, he would not be averse to a repeat performance. She smiled again, and this time held in a giggle. covering it all in her bent knees thinking about Bastion and his kiss.

"So, what did you learn of the Count's evening? Did he learn anything?" Deidra, not as asleep as Aisling thought asked from behind.

Aisling turned her chair partially around, "I thought you were asleep,"

"Well, obviously not now," Deidra commented dryly, but looked hard at Aisling and took a large deep breath. "You bedded him." She accused.

"We bedded each other." Aisling defended herself, "I merely helped the situation a long."

Both the girls laughed, and Aisling joined Deidra on the bed like a million times in their lives as sisters.

"Well?" Deidra asked.

"It was magical. I have never felt so cared for or protected, or..." her sentence trailed off. Deidra was far too perceptive and once she had an inkling about something would not let off until ferreting the truth. "The physical aspect of bedding is as we have read in books, but the feel of it is nothing you would expect." Aisling finished with hot cheeks and even hotter desire reliving it again

"Well, are you going to marry him?" Deidra asked.

"Marriage? Where did that come from. You know we decided I would be the one to care for father."

"I just thought the Count more of a gentleman than that." Deidra said, making Aisling's defenses kick in.

"Don't you dare Deidra. Do not start pestering him about marriage. It is unfair." Aisling protested.

"Unfair? How do you gather it is unfair? He took your innocence–"

"One cannot take something that was freely given. I had no intentions of marrying before we had relations, and I have no more intentions of it now." Aisling hoped her plea rang truer than in her own mind. She could not admit to Deidra the emotional response their lovemaking had. Aisling would not voice the fear that her heart had been engaged, sometime between the first kiss and that glorious climax in his arms. If given breath it would have life and that would lead her down a road of sadness, which she would not allow.

"I–"

"No. Deidra, I do not care what you think. If you would like me to continue to confide in you, you must promise that you will not try to force this matter, either directly or indirectly. Promise." Aisling knew unless she forced a promise from her sister, she might well end up married via a special license before the next sunset.

"Very well, but I do not promise to cease being concerned for your happiness."

"Very well, that I concede." Both women giggled and fell silent for a moment.

"So, did Senor Guaire tell you if he learned anything?" Deidra pressed on about the real reason Bastion was at their house.

"No," Aisling said with a good bit of guilt in her voice. "I am afraid once we kissed, I was lost to my true purpose. He did say he had news, we would talk of it in the morning." Aisling could not look her sister in the eyes, instead fiddling with the lace hem of the night dress. She had botched it up. Had taken her own pleasure over the family's reputation, in more ways than one.

"Don't" Deidra said with compassion, reaching out to take Aisling's hand. "You will not feel guilty for once in your life putting your desires before the family's. There would have been nothing to do with the information the Count got at that time anyway. You deserve to be happy, just as you desire for all of us you know."

Aisling looked at Deidra and couldn't help but smile knowing exactly what she was thinking. "Thank you."

Deidra bent forward and popped a kiss on the top of Aisling's head. "Well, I might as well rise for the day, for if I fall back to sleep now, I might sleep till noon."

"I decided that very thing sitting here." Aisling agreed, and both the girls rose and began their morning routines. Instead of calling for their maids at such an early hour they did what they often would and helped each other where needed.

An hour later the sisters were up and on their way to the parlor. Deidra needed to go over the household books and decided that it would be best completed in the quiet of the morning, then she would be able to have a budget for cook when they sat down to do the meal planning after breakfast. Aisling decided a walk in the rose garden as the sun came up would be a special event she didn't often get to enjoy.

"I shan't be long. I just need some air." She told Deidra as she grabbed a shawl and straw hat hanging by the door. The cool morning air washed over her overly heated cheeks. Could a person expire from blushing? As she meandered around the side of the manor the birds were busy chirping and waking up the world. The dew sparkled in the growing sun rays and the smell of the roses in bloom lay heavy in the air. She loved the gardens in the morning.

As a girl she would pretend they were her own fairy garden filled with magical creatures and wishes. As she entered the gate that closed off the roses from the rest of the gardens a strange scraping noise came from within. As she wended through the rows of red, pink, yellow, and white blooms the noise became louder.

A woodchuck, come to destroy father's work perhaps? If so she would shoe him off and make a note to tell the gardener to take care of it. Walking up the center row and turning left, Aisling stopped short when the source of the scratching was not a furry, plump woodchuck, but a fully formed hooded individual. A man she could not see because of the hood and dark cloth wrapped around his face.

"What do you think you are doing?" Aisling demanded, with no thought that no one in the household save Deidra was even up, much less knew she was outside.

The assailant stopped digging and turned with menace in his dark eyes, lifted the shovel over his head with the intent to silence her. She remembered in that second most men thought it took a veritable army to get a woman presentable for the public, he did not know that every servant in the house slept still. She screamed.

With every last bit of energy in her body Aisling screamed long and hard. The surprise in his eyes satisfaction alone, but the fact the black guard dropped the shovel where he stood and took off running out of the garden took her heart beat down a notch. She ran after him still screaming at top volume, hoping to keep him moving and not looking back to see no one coming to her rescue, and to see if she could determine which direction he headed in.

To her surprise just as the black guard disappeared in the woods three groundskeepers, and two grooms came running from the back part of the property, and Deidra had flung the parlor window wide on the side of the house facing the gardens.

"Whatever are you screaming for?" She asked

"A–A man. There was a man in the rose garden digging something. When I came upon him, he made to hit me with a shovel." Aisling got out as all her nervous energy and fear spilled forth. Tears hot on her now cold cheeks trailed down. Reaching up to wipe them away with a hand that shook so badly she poked herself in the nose.

"I'll round up a party, we'll go a huntin' Miss Aisling. Don't you worry boot a thing." The head gardener said, as he turned and yelled for more men and ordered one of the young grooms to escort Aisling back into the house. To her surprise, Bastion appeared. One moment he wasn't and then he was like she had conjured him.

"I will escort Miss Lightowler back in. That will be all." The groom bowed, not having a reason not to and left them alone.

Aisling shook harder, visibly now, as the tassels on her shawl danced around. "No, we need to see what he was digging for." She wrapped the shawl more tightly to keep out the now uncomfortable cool morning air. She should go inside, but with Bastion as a comfort she felt protected, standing there in his breeches, open shirt with no coat, and bare feet. Bare feet. Bastion ran outside of the house in his bare feet.

If they returned to the house now, Aisling might not stop off in the parlor, but continue on to Bastion's rooms and his bed. A desire to be wrapped in his arms washed through her. If she turned into him and rested herself on his large chest, his arms would come around and remain there until safe to return to the real world. "Here, over here." She directed leading Bastion and the others who gathered deep into the rose garden giving time and space to her shattered nerves to regain control. "There." She pointed.

Bastion strode by, stepping over the shovel that would have surely meant Aisling's death had he taken the time to wield it. stepping around the shovel Aisling peered around Bastion's arm as he looked into the shadows.

"Hand me the shovel love–" he said, looking around to see if they were alone while his cheeks blazed. A warm feeling filled her to hear the endearment but rallied and gabbed the shovel handing it over.

After a few scoops of well fertilized earth they heard a distinct clunk. The found something. "What is it?" Aisling asked? "And, was he putting it in there or taking it out?"

"Good question, but I am not sure, we will have to see what is in it." Bastion answered as he knelt to pull the decorative jeweled box out of the ground. It was quite ornate and expensive. Bastion stood up and turned. Aisling couldn't wait to see its contents. All fear evaporated with Bastion's presence and the new find.

"Well?" she prodded, but Bastion just tucked the box under his arm and took hers in his free hand turning them toward the house.

"You need some tea and food. You are still shaking and probably in shock. You need food, or you may faint."

"Pish, I am not one to swoon, Senor Bastion," she assured him and his haughty male attitude.

"I did not say you were, Miss Lightowler, but I have seen men, strong, healthy men go into shock and pass out. Getting food into you will help." He explained not stopping just moving them inside. Once there, he led her into the parlor where Deidra, who had apparently seen them coming had a pillow all set with a blanket ready to cover Aisling with.

"Sit." Bastion directed as he set the box down on the table and went to the desk to get a magnifying glass and note card. The butler came shuffling in, still trying to adjust his collar as he did so. "Ah, good, can you send someone to my room to fetch my leather satchel? It has tools I will need to examine this box."

"Yes, of course Sir." Pilchard answered and turned on his heel and left the room.

"I called for tea and cakes to be brought round." Deidra said.

"Good, the sooner she eats the better." Bastion answered gruffly.

Deidra sat down next to Aisling on the couch and fluttered about her as if she had been plucked from death's very hand. Aisling hated being made a fuss of, and more so now that she had taken care of the matter and saved herself.

"Deidra, stop. I am perfectly fine now. There is no reason to fuss so. You are worse than mother." Deidra sighed, but rose and moved to the table next to Bastion to better see the box.

"What is in it?" Aisling asked anxious to see if it had anything to do with the murder.

"I do not know yet, I haven't opened it. I must first examine the box," Bastion explained as she suspected he would explain something to a child. "I do not think he was digging this up, I think he was putting it in the ground." Bastion said, which surprised Aisling and Deidra by the look on her face.

"Whatever for?" Deidra asked before Aisling could muster the energy. To her chagrin the energy drained from her the longer she sat in the relative safety of the parlor, with the small fire warming the room. However, would not admit to being lightheaded, but hoped the tea tray arrived soon.

"Here you are sir," Pilchard said, as he walked in the room at a good pace considering his age. He had a bundle of tools for Bastion. Pilchard handed them off, took one look at Aisling, clucked his tongue and disappeared. Deidra glanced over at Aisling and sucked in a breath.

"You are as pale as one of father's roses. You need to go lie down."

"No, I do not. I need some tea and food and I need to know what a stranger was doing in our garden." Aisling protested. Pilchard returned with the tray.

"I thought I would bring it up for you Missus, since I was down there myself." Pilchard explained, bustling back into the room, but the look of concern on his face told Aisling he sped things up a bit.

"Thank you, Pilchard. I am indebted." Aisling thanked the servant.

"Not at all Miss, happy to help. Here you go, just as you like it." Pilchard handed Aisling a cup of tea with cream and honey. Aisling would have liked the cup to not rattle, but to her dismay her hands would not stop shaking. She managed to take a long draw without spilling it. The warm sweet beverage comforted Aisling as it warmed a path to her belly. The butler handed over a small biscuit with butter and elderberry jam lathered on it. "Eat, you need to get your energy back Miss."

"Thank you, but such fussing is not necessary." biting into the still warm biscuit. The butter had begun to melt, and the elderberry jam had warmed as well. She had never eaten anything better, or perhaps a condition of over active nerves, but it tasted like home and safety.

Leaning back into the cushions and letting her head fall back felt comforting. Soon she would feel better but, in the future, would make sure a riding whip would complete any ensemble when venturing out by herself.

"Are you feeling better?" A deep, honeyed voice, very close

had her eyes shooting open." Bastion knelt at eye level, studying her.

"I am perfectly well, thank you." Aisling answered.

Bastion grunted at that, reaching out touching her forehead.

"Oh, for the love of... I do not have a fever. I got startled is all. Now that I have eaten and have a good strong cup of tea in me, I will be perfect."

Bastion pierced Aisling with a sharp look, but this time it was with the promised desire burning in his dark eyes. It sent a chill down her body and made her twitchy and nervous for a host of other reasons. Was this what life would be like every time they made eye contact?

Bastion rose and went back to the box. He examined it and used a brush to clean off the loose dirt still covering it. "This box may be old, but it hasn't been buried for so long."

"How do you know?" Aisling asked from the couch around another bite of biscuit.

"The dirt brushes off easily and is not imbedded in the cracks. Even on the gems the dirt falls away like it was newly thrown on it. I can say with some conviction that our mystery trespasser was in the process of attempting to bury this when you came upon him."

"Yes, well whatever, he was very determined." Deidra commented as Constance and Maria came hurrying into the room. "What happened? Did you get hurt?" They both asked at once.

Aisling recounted the incident and they all moved closer to the box, when Bastion got ready to open the lid. The lid opened easily with no resistance to even the squeaking that old hinges were known for.

"Well," Maria asked in a breathless voice.

"We have a ring." Bastion took the beautiful emerald ring

from the box, and even in his large work weathered hands it looked large.

"Is that the one Corinthia was given?" Constance asked, leaning in to see the craftsmanship for herself.

"It appears so," Aisling agreed, heart sinking a bit. The ring had been lost and assumed destroyed in the fire, but apparently it never made it to the manor.

Bastion looked at the ring, but then set it aside and drew out an old piece of foolscap with the watermark for the paper just visible in the corner. "It is a nota," He looked up correcting his Spanish to English, "note"

"What does it say?" Aisling asked, but feared she already knew the answer.

"It is dated the day before the fire." Bastion said scanning the note. "It is from Corinthia explaining why she has to do what she is about to do." He continued reading.

"Well, that is that." Deidra spoke softly with defeat too clear to hide. "We are ruined. The lot of us."

Maria and Constance sat back down in the occasional chairs behind them, silent.

Aisling had nothing to add, but she watched as Bastion continued to examine the letter. Not the words, but the paper and perhaps the ink. She wasn't sure. The room fell silent as the burden of what this box meant settled on them all. Meanwhile, Bastion seemed to ignore the atmosphere and continued to look the paper over carefully. "Can you bring me candle?"

"What?" Aisling asked not sure she heard him correctly.

"Candle, with a match please." He said without looking away from the paper.

Aisling rose and, thankfully was no longer shaky on her feet. She crossed to a table and opened the drawer pulling out a candle and moving to the mantel grabbed the matches. "Here,"

"Thank you, Deidra do be a help and close the curtains. Constance, shut the doors, will you?" He continued to stare at a spot on the letter. "Aisling light that candle will you and hand it over here." She lit the candle and handed it to Bastion, leaning in to see too. He held the candle under the paper, but not close enough to light it on fire. Aisling and her sisters watched as a smile broke across his face. He pulled the candle out from under the page and set it in its holder on a nearby table.

"There is a lot of study on the age of paper. The monks and Catholic church have been working on ways to date documents based on the paper for years." Setting the candle in its holder.

"Oh?" Aisling said, immediately thankful for this stranger, who traveled across a continent to help them.

"Yes, and unless you are part of the antiquities community you would not be familiar with some of the more obvious tells that a piece is not as old as one might claim. See here, the watermark?"

"Foolscap." Deidra answered.

"No. It is not. See, the true watermark has the foolscap and bells turned at this angle," spinning the paper to show the women how the barely visible stamp would be upright if the paper were turned. "Instead," he turned the paper again to the top of the paper, "It is at this odd angle not upright, but not upside down either.

"Well, couldn't it be a misprint?"

"It could, but it is unlikely. As the printers were very meticulous about the positioning of the watermark, as an example of their quality of work. Also, I can rub the ink off this letter if I rub hard enough. A letter that was penned over 80 years ago would not still be damp enough to rub from the page. It would have long seeped into the paper and any ink left would have dried."

Maria and Constance clapped their happiness that this was a fake. Relief washed over Aisling at the thought they were not yet ruined, but the question of who wrote this note and why were they trying to bury it at their home hung in the air?

"Can any of what you claim be proven?" Deidra asked with a cold edge. "Or are we going to be made fools of if we try and use this to our benefit?"

"Deidra." Aisling chided. Her tone alone was rude, but the words were beyond.

"No, it is perfectly understandable. Deidra has every right to be concerned, but yes. I assure you it can be proven. The people who can do that are not at all close by, but if it comes to it the note could be sent to Oxford." Aisling watched Deidra's shoulders slacken a bit at the news. "I do not believe we will need to take things that far, however. Whoever the person is trying to frame your ancestor for a murder I do not believe she committed, knows very little about antiquities.

"If he did he would have done a much better job at this debacle." Bastion refolded the letter and set it back into the box. The ring left forgotten now held his attention. "I also believe this is not the ring it is meant to be taken as." Bastion said considering the ring at every angle. "Do you know if there is a rendering of the original anywhere?"

Constance cheered and made a funny squealing noise, "There is." She stated, as she clapped her hands together and held them close. "Corinthia's parents commissioned a portrait be painted of their daughter before the wedding to be hung in the family gallery. It was completed only days before the fire, and Viscount Lightowler never allowed it to be hung in the gallery, because of the pain it would have caused his wife. "

"Is she wearing the ring?" Bastion asked.

"I believe she is."

"Pilchard!" Deidra called, and the butler came shuffling down the hall and into the room.

"Yes, Miss?"

"Pilchard, do you know where the last portrait of Lady Corinthia is stored?" Aisling asked.

"Why, yes miss I do."

"Ah, we need to have it brought here immediately." Constance interjected.

Pilchard blinked, looked around the room, blinked again, "Here? To this room, Miss?" He asked with unease.

"Yes." Aisling assured him. "Where is it?"

"Tis in the attic Miss. I will have to find Mrs. Hascomb and at least two footmen, for tis awful heavy and large."

"That is fine Pilchard, thank you." Aisling assured him. The butler left. The request did not sit well, but now all they only had to wait to see if in fact the ring was a fake.

CHAPTER 13

*A*fter twenty minutes a footman came down and explained the task would take longer than first expected. It seemed a locked door and a missing key the major roadblock. Mrs. Hascomb was searching, and they would come back with updates. Maria and Constance had grown board of waiting. Constance asked to be notified in her studio when the painting arrived, because she had been working on a piece and didn't want to lose the morning light. Maria noticed a new issue of the London Society pages and headed off to find some cakes and a quiet place to pour over the latest fashions and to take notes about alterations she could make to all their dresses to keep them up to snuff with London.

Deidra sat back down at the writing desk to finish going over the accounts and then perhaps go talk to cook about a shopping list before she was called back to the parlor to examine the painting.

Aisling sat on the couch for some moments in silence not sure what to do next. She supposed that a change of clothes was in order, since the first gown of the day did not fair well, being crushed and dampened by her ordeal, but before she could say anything Deidra commented. "Your dress is in great need of a wash dear sister. It appears that you were what that blackguard was attempting to put in the ground."

"Thank you for noticing," Aisling retorted feeling a bit self-conscious and stealing a glance at Bastion picking up his tools.

"I am merely suggesting while everyone in the house is otherwise occupied it would be a desirable time to get out of that." She said with a naughty little smile. Aisling turned pink if the heat prickles were any indication. Looking again at Bastion who wore a mask of indifference. Did he hear Deidra's jib and not understand it, or did it not affect him?

Oh. Aisling sighed to herself. This was ridiculous. Bastion owed her no promises of more stolen kisses or sensual nights and she should not be looking to him for more.

"I am going to return my tools, and find some breakfast, as the excitement did not allow me time to find any food this morning. I will see you ladies in a while." He rose, bowed his head and left the room. Well apparently he either did not hear, understand, or was not interested. A tightness covered her chest and she all of a sudden wasn't as worried about the state of her skirts, but with lack of anything to do. Not even able to sit back and observe Bastion now, she might as well change.

Aisling rose. "I guess I will go change and see if I can tame my hair."

"I'm sorry, did I miss speak?" Deidra asked looking up from her needlework. She liked to pick at Aisling, but never would hurt intentionally.

"Who on Earth knows," Aisling said with exasperation. "I most assuredly have no knowledge of what he is thinking, and it is driving me to distraction. And the fact that it is driving me to distraction is driving me to distraction. I cannot live not knowing what to say, what to do, how to act." Aisling put a hand on her forehead as she was wont to do when she got frustrated.

"Just be you. He did not attempt to bed any of us, he only wanted you." Deidra said.

"You are right. That is all I can be. We made no mention of a repeat of anything, so I should just assume our affair is over. Thank you, sister." Aisling said before squaring her shoulders and walking out of the room.

As Aisling nipped passed the dining room doorway, a large hand snaked out and encircled her elbow. Aisling only jumped for a moment until realizing it was Bastion. He had a Danish in his mouth and another in his free hand, but the hand around her elbow, once she was fully in the room laced through her arm and tugged her tight to him. He swallowed the bite of Danish and set the other one aside.

"Are you quite recovered from your ordeal?" Bastion asked looking her over.

"Oh, yes, yes, quite fine. I just needed some food as you said. I hadn't eaten either so the excitement on an empty stomach was not wise." She babbled.

"Did he strike you?" Bastion asked, and Aisling saw his face change into something filled with anger.

"No. I did not give him the opportunity. I would not remain still, and I began to scream. We were too close to the house to be alone long."

Bastion's shoulders relaxed as did the hard plains of his face. They were close, so close Aisling could hardly breathe. His arm pulled her again until they were touching. He was staring with as much interest as he had shown his Danish a few moments ago. Heat filled her body when she thought of him doing that very thing only hours earlier. She wanted to say something witty, some repartee' that would suit the situation, but what did the lamb say to the lion before it was eaten?

"Come." Bastion growled, taking her hand and walking deeper int the room toward the silver and linen closet. The door swung only wide enough to usher her into the darkness. Aisling heard the door shut as she was plunged into darkness. His presence filled the space surrounding her.

The closet was large as closets go, Aisling had always thought, but perhaps not so much if your plan is to enter it with a behemoth such as the 4th count of Lugar de Sueno'. Once her eyes adjusted, she could see the outline of his face and broad shoulders. "What are you about Count?" She asked.

"Why Miss Lightowler. I plan on taking advantage of you in the silver closet while all the servants are busy, as your sister suggested." He said low in his voice so close that his breath with every word fluttered the wayward curls around her face.

Aisling didn't know how to respond to such a bold proclamation, so she remained silent and waited. It wasn't but a breath's time that he lowered his mouth to hers in a hungry kiss, that quickly escalated to his hands caressing up and down her back. He cupped one breast with possession. Even through the layers of muslin his hand was hot making her nipple tighten and pucker. "Oh, mmmmmm." Aisling knew she was not making any coherent sense, but the sounds were pulled from her soul by the physicality of his touches.

"Shhh, love. You will get us caught for sure, then our play will be stopped. At least until the night." Lulling her with his words.

His kiss meandered along her jaw and up into the hollow just below her earlobe sending another wave of shivers to ever raw nerve. She didn't care what he did or where, just wanted more of his touch. bending to give him access to her neck and as he took it, his free hand slid up and undid the bow at the center of the dress under her bosom. The dress loosened sliding off the other shoulder exposing the yet to be occupied breast to the cool air of the closet.

"Bastion" She whispered.

"Yes, love?" He asked in a thicker Spanish accent than she had heard before.

"Don't stop."

"You are going to drive me crazy. You smell of citrus and roses, like a sparkling wine one drinks in the heat of the day to be refreshed. And you taste–"

"Mmmm, she could only make mewling noises because logical discord was beyond her.

"You taste like a rainstorm." He finished bending to lave one puckered nipple. She wove her hands into his thick mane of hair that had yet to be tether back in his haste.

Bastion pulled her closer and held her. Aisling absorbed his warmth and security.

"When I heard you scream this morning. I knew it was you."

"Well," Aisling attempted to continue the conversation, but wasn't sure how the dratted man could converse in the middle of their current situation "I will not be so cavalier as to say I was not set on edge by the whole nonsense. I never thought we would come to harm in such a way. A drunk tavern visitor deciding to be done with the nonsense and just get rid of the line, yes, but in my father's rose garden, by a hooded figure. Never"

He captured her mouth again in a passionate kiss, sending her senses swirling. He pulled away only long enough to move to the other ear and nibble. How on Earth did one learn that an ear was so sensitive? She mused

"What do you remember? Did you see his face?" Bastion asked, while trailing kisses down until his tongue found the hollow at the base of her neck. Aisling giggled or groaned, she wasn't sure, but didn't care.

"I ah, well. The shadows made it difficult. That time between day and night. The man stood as tall as you. Oh, my–" She attempted to answer but became distracted by his hand finding its way to her thigh. He pulled at the knee to bring it high on his hip. She could feel his erection at her core then.

"Bastion!" she said with excitement.

"Shhh. Did you see his face?" He asked, rubbing against her driving their desire higher. "What did the bastard look like?"

"Mmm, blond," She moaned as he nibbled on her collarbone and kissed back up the way he had come. "I–I could see it from under his hood. I think light eyes."

"That's it love," Bastion coaxed with deep gravel in his voice. Bastion was quiet for a moment kissing and dipping his tongue in her mouth. Aisling tasted raspberry Danish and strong tea. Heart pounding, certain a servant would open the door to see about the hammering sound. "Did he seem familiar to you love?"

"Ah," She tried to consider his question, but desire made logical thought fuzzy. "I–I am not sure. Mmmm." lost to his touch.

The realization Bastion had complete control yanked Aisling from the haze. Panic coiled around her throat at the thought. If she started seeing herself as his, when he finally left whether their situation was improved or not, it would break her. Aisling coughed and pushed herself away from his strong, warm, protective chest. lips still burning from their kisses. Breathing hard, but she sensed he understood their time was done.

Bastion kissed her on the forehead, lingering for a bit longer than necessary. "I am relieved you have no ill effects from this morning's ordeal Love, I think I would have come undone had you been injured. That, I will not allow." He moved back and opened the door ajar to peer out. "You go, you need to change and set your hair to rights, I am afraid I did not leave it in any better condition than before we entered the closet. I will wait until you are safely in your room before making my escape.

Aisling looked up at him. He had apparently done this type of thing before. The thought sent a cold chill down her spine and only helped to harden the wall needed around her heart before losing it. "Of course, Count." She said and dipped to slide under his arm and out the door bustling up the stairs before anyone could see. Disheveled hair not the only part that would give away their activities if noticed. Wiping away a tear as she turned the corner at the top of the stairs to find her room.

Bastion waited alone in the dark closet for a good ten minutes before emerging. It was a good thing that he took the time to wait for Aisling to flee. It gave him time to cool his blood. Had he not let the girl escape, they would have made love right there. Even now as heading up the stairs his cock pressed against his pants. It might well scare a maid. The purpose for the closet was to distract Aisling's mind enough to say something her conscious brain would have missed, not to ravish the already traumatized lady. He only meant to kiss until she was otherwise occupied. Bastion never considered being swept away with passion as well. Damn that woman. Nothing but a slip of a thing. Nothing like the Spanish women he had been raised on.

Rounding the corner of the hall and within steps of his room the headache began. It started slow, almost imperceptible, but Bastion recognized it. Right behind his eye the throbbing started It spread up and over the top of his head and back until there a relentless stabbing at the base of his skull began. He was about to have a vision. Bastion picked up the pace and entered his room, just as white light overtook his eye sight and the pain in his head, sent him to his knees with his head in his hands.

A place he had never been, but close by. Aisling stood next to him and they were conversing with a man. The stranger in question turned Standthrope

His jovial smile welcoming, but Aisling did not seem comforted Clinging to Bastion fear coming off her in waves.

Andrew was talking and gesturing to a window. Bastion stomped over and looked out. The image made him recoil. A woman, the same maid in his vision where the manor burned stood outside the window, burned and decaying dressed in clothes that were black with soot where the fabric remained intact, which wasn't much, obviously burned off by the charred edges that remained. Her burned face, and her visage swayed between being seen through fire and being a burned corpse. She didn't speak but gave Bastion the knowledge that it was the blond man, whatever that meant.

When Bastion turned back from the window Aisling stood at the writing desk along the same wall holding a sheaf of paper the same as the note from earlier and a pen with ink dripping from it. Standthrope nowhere to be found but draping over the chair at the desk was a black cape with a hood attached. As he stepped toward Aisling to take her from the place she lifted the pen above her head and thrust it into the portrait of a girl of the manner. This all feeds back to him a voice said. Find him, you have found the cause and the way to protect Aisling.

With a loud gasp and a violent start Bastion was back in his room on the floor, on all fours gasping for breath. He remained concerned his legs would not hold his weight just yet. Something hot covered his lip. Bastion reached up to wipe blood from under his nose. The visions were worsening. As much as Bastion hated the pain and agony, he knew closure would be soon. The box and the information from Aisling must have triggered it. Perhaps the painting would give some answers, but Bastion was not sure another powerful vision today would be wise. He would endure of course if it meant helping Aisling of course.

Forcing his legs to work he rose from the floor. With no way to tell how long the vision had trapped him the importance of making it back to the parlor in good time weighed on him. He went to the basin of water and washed the sweat and blood from his face. Once sure the nose bleed had ceased, a clean cravat was in order. It was also necessary to finish dressing and becoming presentable from his race to the garden this morning. Before leaving, He stuck his head in to check on his nephew, but his tutor must have the boy outside. Considering this morning's events, Bastion wondered on the prudence of letting them out but decided the culprit's desire is to show the Lightowlers as guilty, not get the local authorities here because of a crime. He would skip dinner tonight with the family and have it with Niall. He ate every night with his nephew at home and missed hearing about his day.

Next to see about this painting. The activity in the hall was a good sign. It would not be long before they were able to free the painting from its storage. He left and headed back to the parlor.

Once at the door, excited murmurs rang through the wooden panels before a footman opened the door for him to enter.

"Count, you were right!" Maria was exclaiming excitedly to

him. –More words than she has gifted him with since his arrival.

"I was correct about what part?" He asked stepping over to the painting, propped up in front of the bank of windows letting in the sunlight of the early afternoon.

"The ring," she answered. "It isn't the same. Just as you said." Maria had gone to the painting with the ring from the box and held it next to the one in the painting.

The engravings were not similar in the least on the side of the ring casing. The ring in the painting had delicate Celtic engravings, so specific an art historian would have to agree that the ring was given some importance in the portrait.

"And, look," Constance added as she pointed to two diamonds on either side of the large emerald set in the middle. "This fake doesn't have the diamonds."

Bastion put out his hand and Maria placed the ring in it and he again examined the ring and its setting. There was no place on the ring setting made for a diamond on either side. Bastion held the ring more in the sunlight and noticed the milkiness in the center of the stone.

"Well, either this is the poorest quality stone to ever be given a lady for marriage, or it is not a real stone at all."

"Drat,"

"What on earth are you drating, Deidra?" Aisling asked confused.

"When this nonsense is all over, that was found on our prop-erty and we could have sold it for a hefty sum." Deidra explained, distress clear in her voice.

All the girls laughed, and Bastion could only chuckle and shake his head. How different these women were from each other, yet as a group they complimented each other's strengths.

"Can we call in a local jeweler to confirm that these two

rings are not a like and that this one is fake?" Bastion asked not knowing what access they might have.

"I can have Pilchard call for someone, but it may take more than a day, as we will have to have someone come from Durham or Newcastle. He would know." Aisling said and headed off to find the butler.

Bastion decided to take the opportunity with Aisling not there to escape for the afternoon and do a bit of digging around the local area. He still had not heard from Standthrope with a meeting day and time, until that information came he was at a standstill and there were some other questions, not about the Lightowlers that were plaguing him. The visions every night about the woman burning pried on his mind. Ordering a footman to have a sturdy horse saddled and brought round and Bastion left for his room again to grab his tools. This had to do with his own history he could feel it in his bones. finding answers without causing more stress to his hosts would be preferred because he was certain his own story did not have a happy ending.

CHAPTER 14

The passage from England to Scotland showed little if any distinction for Bastion, except his own heightened sense of belonging and dread. He knew his mother's family had not heralded from Spain or even France originally, but as a boy he never considered Scotland. When either him or his brother would ask, she would say it was a story for another moment, when they were older.

When she passed away Bastion combed through her belongings for any family history but found none. What had happened so long ago that sent fear into their mother and her ancestors?

The road nearly empty as he traveled with his thoughts. Bastion didn't know what lay ahead. However, whatever it was, his family had survived and thrived. Bastion did not know any of his relatives on his mother's side, but she used to speak of several. Perhaps back in Spain he would start doing some research and find his family. If not for him, for his nephew. The idea of going home sent a pain to his chest, because the next thought after going home is having to watch Aisling fade into his memory. Her loyalties were with her family. He was without a family and would never ask the woman he loved to leave hers.

Bastion jerked in the saddle enough to upset the horse who shook the reins and huffed at him, but where had the word love come from? He had bedded her once, almost ravished her in a closet and actually had not even danced with in a ballroom or played cards with her in the evening. They hadn't even known each other for a whole week in person. Love was and should remain the farthest thing from his mind. Thinking on more pragmatic things for the remainder of the trip would be prudent. Love was anything but pragmatic.

Not even a mile more and his head began to throb, and his stomach recoiled. Bastion directed the horse off the main road and down a smaller road to the left. After a few minutes a field came into view. The field from his vision. Turning to the right and there, just as he knew it would be a gravel covered circle. A stone slab stood in the middle with a wooden railing around it.

Bastion dismounted and lumbered with the horse to the edge of the wooden railing. Engraved on the stone slab were three names. Niall Dalais, Caitrìona Dalais Guaire, Sorcha Dalais Creag. At the bottom was a date and the inscription *We shall carry these deaths on our conscious for eternity.*

"Evening, can I be of assistance?" A voice came from beyond the stone that Bastion couldn't seem to take his eyes from. The voice belonged to a man at least ten years Bastion's senior. He was wearing the clothes of a preacher. For the first time Bastion noticed that the circle stood in the church yard.

"Yes, thank you. What can you tell me about this?" He asked attempting to thin out his Spanish accent.

"Oh, well that," The gentleman began with a sadness to his voice. "That is the darkest point in our little town's history I am sorry to say."

Bastion didn't say anything, just waited.

"We had a pastor at our church who had a horrible tragedy befall his family and, in his grief, he accused and convinced the towns people that siblings from a very prominent family were witches." He turned and spit. Were the taste of the words so bad, or perhaps a curse put on a long dead pastor?

"How many siblings were there?"

"Three. A brother and two sisters."

"Were there children?"

"Oh, Lud no!" The minister gulped on his words. "That would have made the heinous act almost unthinkable. Twas' bad enough good people had to suffer because of one man's craze."

"What of their family?"

The vicar stood and looked at Bastion to the point if Bastion was a lesser man he might squirm under such scrutiny by a clergyman. Memories of having his ears flicked by the priests as a boy who would not sit still during mass sprang to life.

"Come with me." he said and turned expecting Bastion to fall into step. "I am vicar Danbury." They ambled toward the vicarage, or so Bastion assumed.

"Bastion." Was all he offered.

"Something tells me there is a Lord attached to that name." The Vicar Danbury looked sideways at him.

"Actually Count. 4th count of Lugar De Suneno." Bastion explained. There was no reason to not share his. Who just nodded knowingly.

Once in the small home Bastion had to take a moment to allow his eyes to adjust. It was cozy, but had seen better days, perhaps for the crazed pastor who liked to burn people–his people. The thought settled in his bones. These were his ancestors. They had given him his power and his brother. The vicar led him to the back of the building which was much longer than Bastion had first thought. In a large storage room, which appeared to house much of the church's belongings both valuable and not so much Danbury shuffled over to a pile in the very back, set apart from the rest, draped with a furniture cloth.

Vicar Danbury pulled the cloth off the pile with care and set it aside. Bastion wasn't sure how Danbury knew what he was looking for because the room was dim at best, and he had not bothered with a candle. It appeared to be a large pile of portraits not unlike those that hung in his family's home. All framed with not inexpensive framing materials. Danbury rummaged through closer to the back and motioned for Bastion to hold the forward-facing stack, so it would not fall.

"Ah, yes here we are" the vicar said after a few moments. With some jiggling and grunting the large portrait came free from its position and the vicar turned to leave the room. Bastion set the others back gently and followed.

They went into a room off the long hall to the right. Bastion assumed his private parlor once the door was shut and the candles lit. Just as cozy as the rest of what Bastion had seen, but this room had a distinct male flavor to it. The colors were dark and rich with the smell of tobacco and brandy. Bastion raised a brow.

"I am a devoted man of the cloth, but in my youth, I was the younger son an Earl in England. Some of my wildness of being a peer has never really left me." He chuckled. "I am of the idea that God will forgive some smoking and drinking, to make up for me spending my life as an Englishman in Scotland." The corners of his eyes wrinkled when the vicar smiled, and Bastion decided he quite liked Vicar Danbury. He wondered for a moment if God would treat a Spaniard living in England the same. Not sure where that came from it was dismissed straight away.

"Fine, now let us have a look. If my memory is not as foggy as I hope it isn't you are about to either be shocked or confirmed in your beliefs." The vicar turned the painting around to the light and Bastion stood in stunned silence.

"Just as I suspected." Danbury said with pride. I knew I had seen your face before.

There on the canvas the portrait of a man. One obviously happy with his life. His dark hair tied in the back and a thick beard covered his cheeks. Peeking out over the bushy black hair were kind, laughing eyes. His brother's eyes.

Bastion had to choke back emotion. Emotion that he didn't understand just yet. This man in this picture could have been him, his brother, or even his grandfather based on the locket painting his mother had kept. The only hint to her family's past.

"Did you know ye were related?" Bastion took a moment longer before tearing his eyes away. "I ah, I wasn't sure." How to explain having visions of his ancestors burning at the stake and drawing him here? He might find a pyre erected in the same spot for him. I have been researching my mother's family since she passed. She spoke little of her heritage and since it is just myself and my nephew left, I wanted to give him the past I never had.

"Laudable endeavor my boy. I am certain he will appreciate the effort." The vicar said laying the portrait against the sofa and went to a cabinet and pulled out a bottle of whiskey. "I save this for special occasions. I am thinking this fall in those ranks."

The two men sat and drank for a bit in silence. Bastion still trying to make sense of it all, but he knew very little save for his visions, what the stone said, and the vicar's story. Asking for more information if he supposedly already did the research seemed foolish. When asking about strangers not so complicated.

"The story goes that all three siblings each had a power, but they did nay use them for bad ever, and did not flaunt them, but the old vicar blamed one of the sisters after his child was still born and from there would not rest until they were all killed." The vicar just began talking and Bastion didn't say anything for fear he might stop. "Tis also said that the husband of one of the sisters and the wife of the brother hid the children from all three and secreted them out of the country and away from the horror that would have befallen them as well if they had stayed." The vicar continued, pouring another glass for each of them. "That is my favorite part of the story." He said and sat back in his chair assessing Bastion.

"This is your clan my boy. If I die tomorrow, I would profess it till my death. Your people. You have come home."

Home.

Bastion's home was Spain. He was a Spaniard, but the word swirled in his mind and a warmth settled in his chest. As of late, he had not been at home in the large empty hacienda that was his family's legacy. To be honest for the size, it fit like too tight shoes. It pinched him everywhere. "How do the towns people feel about this event now, so many hundreds of years later?"

"Harrumph, most think it a tale they tell their children at night to keep them in their beds. The vicar who took the post after the guilty one was banished, unfortunately not until a ripe old age, kept very careful notes to record the whole event including witness accounts. He had the contents of the proper-ties brought here and cataloged, to be kept under safe watch until which time a family member came back to claim them. I believe he was hoping the children would return so the church could apologize. Not that an apology would bring their parents back."

Bastion agreed but appreciated the thought. "Now, what do you plan to do with all this?" He asked after downing his second generous draught of whiskey. Declining with a hand over his glass when the vicar would have poured more. Danbury looked longingly at the bottle but took his guest's que and set it aside.

"Well, I suppose tis yours." He answered.

"I have no proof I am a relation. No papers or family bible. Nothing." Bastion admitted.

"I didn't think you did, for I am certain you were brought here by a force much greater than a legal document were you not?" An edge of understanding clear in his voice.

"Something like that," Bastion said with a smile "yes."

"Thought as much. An extraordinary family, the lot of ya." He said and rose to the desk and took up paper and an ink pen. "I am going to assume yer horse is not able to handle the contents, and it will take us at least a few days to go over the inventory." The vicar admitted.

"I will send someone with a carriage." Bastion said.

"Good, good."

"I will need the address to where here is, however. I didn't exactly have an address myself." Bastion admitted.

"Very well," he said as he scratched down the directions to the little village. "Might I have a contact point for you as well, in case I have a question?"

"Certainly, I am staying with Lord Lightowler at–"

"Lightowler? The horticulturist?"

"Yes."

"Quite a good chap. I know right where he lives. How are

you acquainted, if you don't mind my asking? Lightowler was a genial fellow, but not one to travel to Spain."

"I was solicited by one of his daughters to help the family work out a problem. I am a bit of an expert on antiquities, and ancient mysteries. She read some articles about me and reached out to see if I could clear her family name."

The vicar nodded knowingly, "All these hundreds of years later and still only for good, lad, only for good."

"Pardon my forwardness, but you seem to think you know something about me or about my family that I do not."

"No, my boy. I don't know anything you don't already know, but all will be confirmed when you have finished reading the journals, which I would add has never been open for reading to anyone but the current vicar. Not a soul."

Bastion just nodded and shook Danbury's hand. He left the vicar at the door of his cottage and Bastion went to collect the horse which had wandered to the edge of the field. The sunlight waned. He would not make it back in time to eat with Niall this evening, but his tutor would wait only so long, before having Niall eat and go to bed. Bastion would have to make it up to him. At least the Lightowlers were not sitting around a table waiting for him to appear.

He set the horse back on the road and turned to give one last look at this place of his family. He would be back. The church looked like it could use a new roof and steeple, and the vicar's cottage surely could use some attention. That circle of stone needed something as well. Perhaps a flower garden. Aisling could help him choose just the right plants. His mother used to say that we were put on the Earth to right the wrongs of our ancestors. This vicarage did all it could over the years to do just that and nothing to gain to see it any other way.

As the sun made its final descent on the horizon, Bastion

bent to the business of getting back to the Lightowler's before he got lost, or worse taken upon. He had no idea how safe the roads were at night and didn't want to find out.

He also had a churning need to tell Aisling all that he found out about himself and his family. To tell her he was not so far removed from her family. His family was once Scottish. Did that mean he would have to don a kilt?

CHAPTER 15

"He is a grown man Aisling. He holds the title of Count. I am certain a Count can ride through the countryside unharmed." Deidra chided Aisling as she stood peering into the darkness from their bed chamber window.

"I am aware of that, but he missed his assignation with Niall for dinner and it is now well passed sunset. Anyone who is not familiar with an area should never travel alone after dark. That is common knowledge." Aisling commented back.

She had not been overly concerned when informed at dinner that Bastion would be dining with his nephew, he hadn't spent much time with the boy since arriving, but when Pilchard returned after dinner and told her that the count had not been back from his ride to dine with his nephew, she began to worry.

When she went to check with the tutor, he assured her that Bastion was a loving uncle, but not yet accustomed to keeping a schedule suitable for a young boy and would often be late or miss appointments because he was otherwise occupied. Perez suggested she not worry over much about it.

Aisling had returned to the parlor with the family until claiming a head ache and settling in her room where she could more easily see the road. Now with the full darkness of the night settling in, it would be impossible to see a lone rider with no lantern, so she turned from the window and sat on the edge of the reading chair.

"Where do you suppose he could have gone off to? He didn't mention any new information." Aisling thought out loud.

"Perhaps it had nothing to do with our situation. Perhaps it was just as the tutor told you and a personal matter." Deidra had escaped the family as well and was perched on the bed with a needlework project close to completion draped over her lap.

"He is from Spain just what kind of personal matter could he have in northern England?"

"I have no idea, but honestly unless we wake in the morning and there is still no sign, I shan't worry about him. Whatever trouble Senor Guaire finds will be deserved since he knows the world. Now, do be a dear and sit there worrying more quietly. I am going to sleep."

Deidra set her project on the floor and put out the candle plunging the room into darkness with only the hazy moonbeam from the uncovered window casting shadows about. Aisling watched and knew when Deidra was asleep. They had shared a room and a bed since they were children. Deidra could fall asleep at a moment's notice. Aisling paced again to the window and decided the view was no longer worthwhile, and she might not hear him walk past the bedchamber, so it made more sense to wait in his room. She grabbed her dressing robe, tying it tight and slipped out of the room.

The maid had lit a fire in anticipation for Bastion to return and Aisling stirred it back to life and sat in one of the two chairs by the fire. The man needed a talking to. Bastion had no right to set her nerves on edge as much as he did. No one should have the power to make anybody such a sensory mess. Hot with desire one moment. Angry with fear the next. How was a woman to get anything done? Everything about him bent to the extreme. Why should the emotions he evoked in others be any different?

He was tall, broad shouldered, muscled where she does not remember other men having muscles, His voice sank at least an octave deeper than any male she could ever remember speaking with. Aisling had no other lover to compare his prowess to but would assume he was above the pale in that regard.

Then there were his visions. Nothing about Bastion spoke calmness. She imagined him at his home in Spain Sitting at a large desk suited to a count well loved by all in his care. An endless stream of women were more than willing to drink from the well and be caught up in his chaos. When Aisling considered this, the man she would marry was nothing at all like Bastion.

Her dream husband would be quiet, read often, and preferred good English tea to the stronger coffee. He was always where she would expect him and did not likely to have too much excitement in his life. No, Bastion not wanting marriage worked fine for her. He was not the one. The fire snapped, and the smell of the beeswax candle filled the room as it began to burn low. She curled her legs under her and leaned her head on the side of the chair. She would just wait for him and...

∾

Bastion carried his boots into the house after taking them off outside the stable as not to wake anyone. He hadn't meant to stay and talk with the vicar so long but could do nothing about it now. He returned safe with the horse and made sure it was taken care of. Padding up the long staircase and down the hall passing Aisling's door his steps slowed. Why the sudden urge to share the news of his newfound relations he didn't want to consider just now. Bastion needed his bed and rest before waking in the morning to give his full attention to solving the Lightowler's problem. He was close.

Quietly stepping into his nephew's room, to see that the boy settled in before making his way into his own room. His nephew lay curled up in a little ball. His long dark lashes swept down on his cheek. A cheek that was rosy with health and life. Niall looked so much like his father, so much like their mother's ancestors. Niall would now have a past, and if Bastion had anything to do with it a family as well. He would find them and reunite them all. Bastion bent to leave a kiss on his tousled hair and quietly made his way into his own room. Once the door shut the room plunged into darkness, expected at that hour, but to his right a candle on the table by the fire spit and sputtered in its last attempts to stay lit and in the shadow of that he saw Aisling.

Curled up, not unlike his nephew, but in one of the straight back chairs. Head rested on one arm draped on the side. The hair he had dreams about out of the pins cascading over the chair and just brushing the floor. She had tried to wait up for him. His chest warmed and tightened at the thought of never coming home to an empty bed chamber again. He padded over and knelt down. Once he touched her the illusion would be broken and he wanted to watch Aisling sleep. Bastion was not accustomed to seeing women in that state. She looked younger than she already was with no worry or sadness obstructing that pearly skin. The one drawback to watching her sleep was that he couldn't see those big eyes. Larger than they should be, wide and full of curiosity. They were lighter in the morning and would darken to frosty gray when excited about something. Remembering last night, when they were ablaze with desire all bright and the deepest darkest gray like a storm over the ocean and it made his cock react.

He never spent time sleeping with women. Most of the women he bedded in Spain were married, so spending the night in their embrace was not an option. With Aisling his soul screamed to be soothed to sleep every night in her arms and to wake with the feel of her weight across his every morning. Bastion's visions put him adrift and apart from the foundation of Earth, with Aisling holding him tight in their bed, he would have a tether to reality and to the world.

Bastion wanted Aisling. It was a forgone conclusion, but not until she could make that choice with no scandal hanging over them. No fear. Bastion rose and carefully slid his arms under her shoulders and knees and lifted her in one smooth motion out of the chair. She was so small he mused, like the butterflies that flit around the gardens at his home. The air carries them, and they can light on the most delicate of petal without it bending. He could carry her like this to Spain without breaking a sweat. Bastion moved across the room, took a moment to open the door stepping out into the hall and down the corridor stopping at the door of her room. The one she shared with Deidra. He knocked as quietly as possible and waited. After a few moments the door slanted open and a blurry eyed Deidra stood looking up at him.

It only took a moment for her to realize the situation. "Oh" she whispered and stepped back opening the door wide to allow him and his parcel in.

"Apparently, she tried to wait up for me." He whispered over the top of his head, the smell of lemon and raspberries from her hair filled his nose.

"She was waiting up to scold you," Deidra said with humor in her voice. "Here." Deidra motioned to the bed and pulled down the covers. Bastion laid Aisling down.

"Scold me? Whatever for?" He asked stepping back and letting Deidra cover her. Aisling rolled to one side and snuggled in with a sleepy murmur.

"She didn't think you should have been out so late."

His Aisling would always scold him he thought to himself and it made him smile. Many an afternoon, or evening would pass with her finger wagging at him for some mistake or reckless behavior if they were together. So long as he had a naked Aisling in his bed at night he would be more than happy to take her ire.

"Whatever is so funny?" Deidra asked now fully awake.

"She is going to have quite a rage when she wakes realizing she was thwarted." Bastion said, knowing the actual train of his thinking was not for mixed company.

"Yes," Deidra agreed with a smile. "Have you eaten?" She asked, putting on her dressing gown and slippers.

"No, I have not. I am famished." Bastion said realizing for the first time tonight that he hadn't eaten since earlier that morning.

"Come, there is no sleep for me now until I get something to eat." Deidra said as she breezed past and out of the room.

In the kitchen Deidra handed him a candle stand and the stove matches. He went to the hearth and grabbed the flint to light the match and proceeded to light the candles casting a soft warm light in the room. By the time he joined Deidra at the work table with the lit candles she had gathered what he could only assume were the leftovers of dinner. Some type of roast meat, boiled rosemary parsnips, peas, and hard cheese with slices of crusty bread. They sat in companionable silence and ate their fill. Bastion hadn't realized just how famished he was.

"Thank you. I am hungrier than I thought."

"Of course." Deidra answered, but he sensed she wanted to say something else. Either fear of being in a kitchen at night while the whole house slept, or fear that she would be rude stopped her. None of the Lightowler girls were fearful of much they might encounter in life.

"You have a question, or a criticism. Please, share." Bastion prodded.

Deidra looked at him head cocked to the side. "You love her."

Bastion knew it wasn't a question. It was an observation, but how could she know? He had been at the house short of a week. He would not answer to a person something not even imaginable.

"Are you going to take her away from us?" She didn't even stop to allow him to answer. "You will have a bugger of time doing it. Not that Aisling would miss us all so much, but because she feels it is her duty to care for father if mother doesn't return. If mama was home Aisling would not think twice to leave with a man she loved, I am sure of it."

Bastion let that digest along with his beef. "Do you think your mother will not return?" deciding on the safer of the topics on the table.

"Who's to say with mama. It devastated her when we were cut by all those who used to call her friend. She loves Papa and us but seems to be enjoying the time with my aunt. If I thought there was a chance of one of us being whisked away to Spain to live out our days and not see her as often, Mama might be inclined to come home if only to say goodbye." Deidra said her tone dropping to a conspiratorial level.

"Would she stay then?" Bastion asked, again ignoring the unspoken question about his intentions.

"Perhaps, but after Aisling was gone she would not know until there would be no logical reason for her to return."

"What would happen to your father?"

"I will be here." Deidra answered flatly.

"Don't you care to marry?" Didn't most women care to marry? Wasn't that their primary goal? He couldn't walk into a parlor in Spain without marriage minded mothers foisting their daughters in his way. The same must be true in England.

"Yes, of course, but a great deal of that depends on how this turns out, but I do not intend to marry into a title."

"Why not?" Bastion asked shock evident in his tone.

"I grew up in a house filled with love, but sometimes little else. My father was the eldest son and his mother made sure he wanted for nothing. His every whim catered to. Papa was never taught that which Papa did not care to learn, so he learned about flowers and plants. My mother was an only daughter and caught papa's eye when only 15. Neither of them knew anything about keeping a household running. There were many evenings when the cook did not have enough food to feed all of us. Many nights we went cold because father had forgotten to tell someone to order more peat for the stove." She sat telling of her childhood, Aisling's childhood, voice heavy with emotion. He couldn't imagine Aisling having to go hungry or freeze. He would not allow it.

"Not all men of rank are as callous with their duties, in fact most are not." Bastion reassured her.

"Oh, I know that. I knew that as a child as well, but what I can't get passed is the utter disregard for anything beyond them and their station. Please, do not think I resent my father. If anything, I resent my grandmother and grandfather. Papa is loving and kind when he thinks of it and would never do anything intentionally to hurt anyone. my father just assumes life will take care of itself, because he has never had to think otherwise. I do believe that is a prevalent attitude among the peerage."

Bastion couldn't argue with that. Many of the Landed men he was familiar with in Spain knew nothing of the plight of their workers or poor farmers. And with the wars they have either become more preoccupied away from their lands or have become stingier with their help and support for fear of economic downfall. Bastion's father would send the boys out into the fields with water, and once a month they were charged with delivering baskets for those most destitute or elderly on their property. It forced the boys to know the tenants, and care about them. Bastion hoped it would never come to it, but he was certain, he would starve before anyone in his charge went hungry.

"Perhaps, but those men are easy enough to spot and fend off." He sauntered over to a platter on the shelf along the back wall and took an apple to eat with his hard cheese.

"Possibly, but I have my sights on a man who knows the value of a hard day's work and the money that comes from that. One who can handle the funds of a Duke, so obviously his family will never go cold or hungry. You can have the Duke." Deidra stated, popping her last spoonful of peas into her mouth.

"You want to marry a solicitor?" Bastion asked incredulous. He had never known a young lady who's dream it was to marry a solicitor. He chuckled and shook his head.

"What?" Deidra asked affronted. "A solicitor is educated, and most likely a younger son or from lower gentry. Will make a livable wage and if good at what he does will be secure in his older years." She defended herself.

"Not very romantic." Bastion pointed out.

Deidra snorted. A lady actually snorted in his presence. Bastion thought.

"Romance does not put food on the table, a roof over your head, or peat in the fire," she reasoned. "That is why you need to take Aisling away with you. She–You and she have a chance at love and as much as it surprises me to say, I believe you are one of those paragons you speak of in the peerage. You must clear our family name, fall in love with Aisling, and take her far from here so she can live in love." He could hear the emotion, but Deidra did not let it spill over. She quickly picked up the feast without another word and left him sitting in the kitchen a half-eaten apple in his hand and an edict from his apparent sister-in- law to be.

CHAPTER 16

*A*isling had not been so put out in a long time, more so in fact than when the family started being left out of the social events. She stood in front of the mirror pinning up her hair for the third time, because for some foolish reason it hadn't looked good the first two. Awaking not in Bastion's room she realized she must have fallen asleep and Bastion brought her here missing the chance to scold him "Oh, for the love of–" She cut out throwing the brush on the dressing table and turning from the unmanageable mass of hair. It wasn't her burden to look at herself all day, so why should it matter? To add to an already foul mood her stomach growled reminding her of breakfast. Deidra must be somehow to blame because she never left the room first in the morning.

Aisling decided since it was her own fault for falling asleep, there was no reason for confronting them at the breakfast table. She plastered on a benign smile and squared her shoulders. When Aisling entered the breakfast room it was filled with animated conversation and clanking silver and glasses. Her eyes met Bastion's as she made her way around the table to the buffet. He nodded and smiled. Aisling returned the gesture, but held her expression plain, until the wastrel leaned back in his chair and she noticed where he was sitting. Directly behind him was the door to the silver closet.

Aisling's cheeks blazed with heat a mix of embarrassment and remembered passion. He only nodded once more and reached up to stretch and leaned his hands on the door behind his head.

"Aisling! Watch yourself!" Constance screeched as Aisling, not watching where she was going stalked right into her sister. Luckily, Constance had seen the impending accident and swung a full plate to the side. "Ouch! You crushed my toe." She complained.

"Oh dear, Constance I am sorry. I should have been watching where I was going."

Constance grumbled something about too many sisters and found a seat. At least now there was an excuse for the blush that continued to burn her from neck to eyebrows she thought. Aisling gathered a breakfast plate and found a seat next to her father.

"Morning Papa. How are you this morning?" asking as she did every morning, it was absolutely not to avoid Bastion.

"Fine, fine. And you dear?" Her father asked in return.

"Very well thank you Papa. What do you have for plans for today?" She asked.

"Well, nothing it appears as exciting and potentially eventful as our guest I think." He answered. Well, so much for avoiding Bastion.

"Oh, Count Guaire, what do you have for plans today?"

"A missive was sent this morning. I will be meeting with the person did not have a chance to tell you about yesterday before your encounter in the garden. I met someone at the card party who may know someone that may recollect what happened. They have set up a meeting today. I am hoping to start piecing things together."

"And," Maria broke in, "There was also a note that the jeweler will be here around noon."

"Really?" Aisling asked shocked. She was certain they would have to go farther afield to find one with a reputation.

"Yes, Miss When I asked in town about a reputable jeweler in the area, told me that a man from New Castle arrived at Lord Franklin's estate. It seems he is having his wife's jewels valued. I took the liberty of sending a rider over requesting if the man had the time." Pilchard explained while pouring more tea for the table, except Bastion who got strong coffee he brought with him from Spain. Her mind wandered to her thoughts last night about over bearing men. Even his morning drink smells strong and too powerful. She caught herself before he noticed.

"Ah, thank you Pilchard."

"I am predicting we will be restored in society before the Laverty's summer ball." Maria crooned as she could barely sit for her excitement.

"That may well be but let us not get ahead of ourselves. This problem did not make itself in a day, so we should not assume it will be fixed so either." Aisling needed to calm everyone's expectations.

"What are you doing today, Miss Lightowler?" Bastion asked, he deep tones vibrating across her nerves and sending heat below her belly.

"I have some inventories to take care of and—"

"Will you be counting silver?" The dratted louse asked with a whole host of inuendo and promise in his voice.

"No." She snapped, trying to look down enough so no one

would see her blushing. "The silver is quite fine as it is. I will be doing inventory of our medical supplies. It has been over six months and I need to see if there are any remedies that we need to make more of."

"Oh." Bastion answered over his tea cup filled with coffee a devilish look in his eyes. A look that sent even more heat rising through her body. A look that said he wanted to lay her out on the breakfast table and feast. Oh Lord, how could she ever live with a man who looked like that over the toast? Should a husband ever look at his wife so? A proper woman would be offended Aisling thought, but the longer their eyes were locked, the more she liked it. Bloody hell. She was going to expire over the poached eggs if this went on much longer.

"Well, I will look forward to a recap of what you find out at your appointment Count, and–" Did Deidra just kick Bastion under the table? No, surely not, she was seeing things. "And, I will make sure Pilchard lets me know when the jeweler arrives. I would like to be present when he examines the ring."

Aisling rose and hoped she left the room at what appeared a calm and relative pace, but her heart beat so hard, she could have been at a dead run and wouldn't have been surprised.

Aisling stood in the servant's hallway in the back of the manor with the door to the medical closet swung wide. She was trying to tally all the supplies and decide if anything needed to be purchased, made, or found before the growing season for many of the herbs was over.

She had lost count on the jars of salve for cuts three time and added it to the list for five more anyway. She reasoned if there were enough for her to lose count, they were not close to running out, but should stock up for the winter months.

She squinted reading the faint label on a vial of clove oil. Last winter when Deidra had suffered from such a horrible tooth ache they had been given the clove oil, by a neighbor. One that now would not even wave to them as they passed each other on the lane. Aisling would have to look into purchasing cloves and extracting the oil, because it had worked so well. She would make it herself and even make extra to return to her neighbor.

Thoughts of Bastion would float across her mind and she would be lost again. Anger had been a strong companion last night, but now Aisling wanted the pressure of his arms around her. Then there was the anticipation of hearing what the witness had to say. Not daring to trust luck and trusting the people in the community even less, Aisling decided this knot of emotions might kill a woman if not careful. At one time those in the community were a source of comfort believing they could go to them in a time of need. Aisling would never be held to that illusion again. It was necessary to regain their place in local society for the sake of her sisters' dreams of marriage, but she would never go to another ball with its twinkling candles and bubbly drinks and see anyone the same.

Coming back to her task at Hand they were getting low on linen strips and bandages.

"There you are. I was looking everywhere for you." Maria came up the hall making her jump so badly she almost dropped the jar of oak bark used for medicinal tea. They could not afford to lose even a piece as it was expensive to purchase.

"Oh, Maria!" she scolded. "You scared me, and I almost dropped the oak bark." Had Aisling been counting instead of thinking of Bastion she might have heard her sister's footsteps.

The servant's hallway did not have thick carpeting like the main ones in the house, but Aisling decided that was a moot issue.

"Sorry," Maria answered a bit defensively. "I was coming to tell you the Jeweler is here in the parlor."

"Good, thank you. Is Bas– Count Guaire returned yet?" Her heart lifted a bit in her chest at the thought of him being in residence this afternoon.

"No. I don't suspect he will be back before dinner." Maria answered.

"Very well, I will be there in a moment. Please ask him to wait."

Maria nodded and walked away. Aisling took a moment to listen and had to admit to herself, that she should have heard Maria coming. Sighing for her own foolish thoughts, she put the bark away, glanced at the notes and shut the door. If someone went ill, they would have what was needed to minister to them. She would make a note to go back and reassess in a month's time just in case.

Aisling was the last person in the household to enter the parlor. To her surprise Papa had even left his greenhouse and was sitting in the back of the room feigning disinterest. Aisling had seen her father and Bastion talking at the breakfast table and at other times, perhaps Bastion was helping to make Papa aware of the import of all this.

"Ah, Miss Aisling I presume?" said a man dressed in the top tier of fashion with gray hair and a slight limp as he stepped to greet her.

"Yes, sorry, I am holding you up." She apologized.

"Nonsense, no bother at all. I am Mr. Finnley from Dorset Jewelers. Very glad to make your acquaintance."

"I already thanked Mr. Finnley for coming out when we were clearly not on his itinerary." Deidra said.

"I was intrigued. It is not every day that a jeweler gets called to solve a mystery." He said with a gleam in his eye. "After your note yesterday, I decided to do a bit of digging on my end. I sent a rider back to New Castle to see if we had any part in the construction of the original piece, and as luck would have it we did. We are the oldest jeweler in this part of England, so it stands to reason any commissioned piece that old may well have been through us." He beamed with the pride of his statement.

"That is wonderful. But, I am not sure how that may assist us." Aisling said.

"Oh, but it does a great deal," The jeweler assured her as he bent low to the painting. "See these inscriptions along the edge of the setting? These would have been hand designed, and we actually have the original artist's renderings of them, with the commissioner's initials next to them giving authorization for them to be included."

Mr. Finnley rustled through some papers that appeared very old, but well maintained. "The store manager sent these back with the messenger hoping to aid in my judgement." He pulled out the sheet in question and sure enough the designs on the ring in the portrait were in fact identical to those on the paper, but not at all similar to the etchings on the setting of the ring they possessed. Which he took up and examined.

Aisling and her sisters all stood around Mr. Finnley in anticipation. It was possibly not necessary to prove this ring a fake, as the drawings and the portrait proved as much, but there would be a bit of satisfaction in having more than one proof.

"Fake." Mr. Finnley proclaimed. "This ring is a fake through and through. In fact, if it had been produced almost one hundred years ago, I doubt it would have remained in such good condition, even if housed as the crown jewels."

Constance and Maria jumped up and down with excitement. They now had some proof that someone was framing them even if they were not able to fully prove their ancestor did not kill her fiancé William and herself in a blaze.

"Good news." Viscount Lightowler piped up in the back. He thanked Mr. Finnley as striding from the room, back to his green house.

"Yes, thank you so much Mr. Finnley. You do not realize how much you have helped us." Aisling explained.

"Oh, but I think I do, Miss Lightowler. When I got your message Lord Franklin was curious and shared with me the impending scandal your family is trying to be free of. I do hope that I have helped your cause. I also have all the paperwork from the original piece if you would like to look it over before I leave. I would like to view your father's rose garden and he promised to give me tour if I cared. I can collect the file when I am finished."

"That would be most helpful, thank you. And would we have access to the file if we needed it later?" Aisling asked.

"Well, since the recipient of the ring was a descendent and your father is the heir and would have sole access to any of the pieces connected to your family, yes."

"Thank you. I will have Pilchard bring you to Papa's greenhouse and I will leave these on the desk for when you return." Aisling offered.

The man bowed and followed the butler out of the room. Deidra was the first to get to the papers and began rifling through them. Aisling stood looking over her sister's shoulder. Constance left to go back to her studio and Maria settled on the sofa with a needlework project.

"It says that William, Lord Landry as a gift for his bride commissioned the piece and put the sale in her name so she would own it outright. The markings on the side were Celtic symbols of love and devotion. He paid a huge sum of money for the ring. Oh, Lord Aisling. I'm not sure Papa's estate ever had so much money. Ever."

"Well, the story does say that Corinthia was marrying up in status, which I am sure angered many in the district." Aisling agreed.

Once Deidra had gone through the file to her liking they piled the pages up neatly and left it on the desk for the jeweler to return.

There was nothing for it, but to wait for Bastion's return. Aisling might crawl out of her own skin before this day was over. She wanted him to return with news that would help them, but to be honest wanted him back for a more personal, purely sinful reason. To see him.

She settled onto the sofa next to her sister and tried to read the book of poetry they had found hidden in the back of a shelf when they were cleaning earlier in the month. Father made them once a year clean the library with the help of the staff, just to make an accounting of the books for him. She had been thrilled to find a new book that she hadn't read at least once, but today couldn't concentrate on a word. She flopped the book down on the cushion next to her. What appealed was go outside and take some fresh air, but Bastion had made the Viscount dictate that none of the girls was to leave the house without an escort and she did not want to bother any of the footmen. They all had chores to do and walking aimlessly around the yard behind her not one of them. Deidra had gone back to the book-keeping, Maria finishing a needlework and Constance lost deep in her studio until dinner was called.

"Oh posh." Aisling said rising. There should be no reason why she couldn't walk around the perimeter of the house, careful to keep the manor in view and not take any of the paths. Maria only glanced up a moment at the noise but shrugged and went back to the project. Aisling would not even be gone long enough to be noticed. She just needed to stretch her legs and feel the sun on her face. Breezing through the house and out the far back door as to not rise suspicion about doors opening and closing was the best route.

The sun, high in the sky now, shot warm beams warming her whole body. She knew if Mama were home there would be a talking to about wearing a hat, but she didn't care. Who needed to worry about freckles if one wasn't planning on marriage? Aisling didn't mind freckles.

She strode around the side of the house reveling in the feel of the exertion loosening stiff muscles. Rounding the front of the manor and onto the gravel drive horses thundering up the lane caught her attention. She had to put a hand over her eyes to see. Bastion was leading the groom that he took with him for direction.

Aisling's breath caught and whooshed out of her body. If he was a gorgeous gentleman standing in the breakfast room, he was a god on horseback. His midnight black hair gleamed in the sun and it was impossible not to stare at his legs and how they hugged the horse to guide the beast to a stop in front of her. She couldn't help herself, she smiled and waved.

"What in bloody hell are you doing out here alone?" He bellowed. Her smile was wiped clean and in its place a battle face went in place.

CHAPTER 17

*B*astion was exhausted. He got little to no sleep the night before, had to cope with leaving Aisling at the manor this morning, when his body wanted nothing more than to bring her to his room and strip her down and make love all day. Now, to see the woman of all his current trouble out alone after Viscount Lightowler had expressly forbidden any of the girls to be outside without escort was more than his frayed nerves could take.

The horse had not quite come to a stop and he was off the beast stalking the woman. Her stance only enlivened his protective nature. She had been smiling when she first saw him come up the drive. His heart filled at seeing such a reaction to greeting him. The excitement however faded at the realization the woman he loved stood alone with no escort in sight. Now, the same woman stood with hands fisted at her sides and a mask of true aristocratic rage covered her face. If there had ever been a question of this miniscule woman's birth all one had to do was look at her. Her perfectly straight nose peaked out from under the thickest, longest lashes Bastion had ever seen, which hooded the widest, brightest eyes. Which, at the moment were shooting daggers at what she knew he was about to say.

"Why the blood hell are you outside unaccompanied?"

"I needed air and saw no reason to pull someone away from their work just to indulge my whim."

Her hands had moved to her hips and he was so close she had to look up to see his face, but she held her ground. "Besides, I am much more aware of my surroundings now that I am aware there could be a threat. I have not left the perimeter of the house."

"It is not safe and won't be until this business is laid to rest, and even then, there may be some parties looking for revenge. It is foolish to not take precautions."

"Foolish? Did you just call me foolish?" Aisling asked, bringing herself up to her full height, which Bastion chuckled to himself brought her up to the top of his chest.

"No, I said your actions were foolish." Bastion said, before he realized that was not what he should have said.

"Well, I never. You have no right coming in here and dictating our activity. You have no right."

"Don't I? You reached out to me. You begged me for help." Bastion pointed out.

"I never gave you leave to make such demands on our daily activity."

"No, you did not. However, I am certain you did not think your physical safety was in jeopardy, but we know now that it is in fact, so–"

"I merely wanted fresh air." She pointed out, "and I never left the view of the house. It is not of your concern."

Her scream the day before in the garden had snapped something inside him and he could have ripped fool limb from limb had the chance come to light. A surge of protectiveness unlike any before it scared him. Bastion had spoken to Lord Lightowler after that and convinced him of the seriousness of everything and Lightowler made the dictate. The Lord apparently didn't know his daughters well enough to know they would ignore him.

He looked at Aisling now, color high from righteous rage of being hemmed in. Her chest rose and fell with more force than usual and threatened to burst from the neckline of the sheer dress. His fingers itched to reach up and give the bright blue bow under her breast a tug and watch the rosy mounds spill out into the sunlight. That forced an image of Aisling spread naked in a sun dappled meadow waiting for him. He hardened at the thought. His face must have shown some of what he was thinking, because she took a step back and her expression became weary. Which did nothing to cool his lust.

"We will discuss this later, when we have more privacy." He bit out, aware of the groom behind him messing with the horses waiting for instructions.

"Thank you, Thomas. I won't be needing the horse again today."

"Yes sir. I'll take him down and give him a good brushing. Jus' let me know ifn' ye need anything." And the boy was gone.

When Aisling raised a slender, feminine finger in the air to dress him down, he rose a hand and cut off the tirade. "Come, I have news." Turning quickly not giving her time to argue making straight for the house. Satisfied Aisling was following when he heard delicate stomps behind him. He loved that she was filled with passion. A memory of his father claiming that a woman with great passions was the perfect woman to wed, unless that great passion was turned against her husband.

Bastion smiled at that, because his mother would swat him and make many threats about what she would do if he scorned her and they would laugh, hug, and usually end up leaving the boys alone to find a quiet place to discuss passion more. Bastion wanted that.

They made their way into the parlor and without so much as a greeting Maria jumped up and began to tell him of the jeweler's assessment.

"Didn't Aisling tell you?" Maria asked.

"It had not yet come up in conversation. His grace had to take time to scold me for daring to go against his and father's edict of leaving the house alone."

"Aisling, you went out without telling any of us?" Maria chastised her older sister.

"Don't you start as well, Maria. I am a woman grown and I can walk around my own home if I see fit." Apparently, Bastion thought watching the play of emotions across each woman's face, Maria may feel the need to question her older sister but would not outright argue if Aisling was in a temper.

Bastion let Aisling alone to cool her ire and went to the desk to look at the papers still on the desk waiting for the jeweler, who would be back any moment to collect them. He was satisfied with the assessment coupled with Corinthia's journal, his visions, and today's information he was certain this would be solved soon.

"What did you learn from that old woman?" Deidra asked as she made her way to the sofa next to Maria. The Jeweler made an appearance to collect his things. Bastion spoke with him briefly and waited until he left.

"Well?" prodded Deidra, who shot Aisling a look that received a sigh in return but walked over and sat between her sisters. Bastion pulled the parlor doors almost shut, but leaving just enough for propriety, he made his way back and sat in the only chair in the circle of furniture that might have a chance of holding his weight.

"I met with a Mrs. Tillison. She was the housekeeper's daughter and lived at Landry house when the murder happened."

"Did she remember? She must have been very little would she be able to understand the subtleties of adult relations?" Maria chimed in.

"Mrs. Tillison is currently almost a year passed ninety, so would have been eight or nine at the time."

All three sisters shot each other surprised glances at the woman's age.

"She remembered the young lord very well, said all the other young ladies in the household were smitten with him. Apparently, he used to pick primroses and find her in the laundry as a special gift for his special girl. And no, before you ask, he was just a genial sort of fellow with a kind heart. No more as the youngest servant in the Landry's employ the family treated her less as a maid and more as a poor relation."

"This is marvelous!" Maria clapped.

"Not so fast," Bastion warned "Mrs. Tillison is being forced to tell me a lie. I will ferret out who it is soon enough, but until I do her public story is that she was certain Corinthia was the murderess and has no recollection of the maid who was pregnant."

"That is, it then is it?" Constance asked as she entered the room at the end of Bastion's tale. "We are doomed."

"No, you are not. I have her real story and as soon as I find a way to protect her from the bad seed that is threatening her she will be happy to tell us the truth." He gave Aisling a pointed look and he knew she understood his visions again have led them here. "I will miss dinner this evening and hopefully when I return I will have this all sorted. It will be up to the gossips to spread the truth and you will be back in the good graces of all the hostesses of the county."

"Will you be in danger?" Aisling tried to not have the question sound as choked. but not sure if she succeeded. Her free entry back into society was not important if Bastion was hurt in the process.

"It is nothing overly taxing. I will leave word with Pilchard about the particulars. He will know when to sound the alarm if necessary."

"Pilchard? Why not us?" Aisling asked panic rising in her throat pushing the words out.

"Pilchard, because he has a clear head and will not get the idea to follow me." He answered with a knowing look.

"Humph" was all she could manage at his sharp retort. "Well fine. I think that is enough excitement for one day. I think I shall go take a nap." Aisling stated, hoping to sneak away with her emotions and fears to sooth herself.

The others didn't seem to notice and sat discussing the updates and who's upcoming event they would choose to attend first. Aisling's foot hit the top stair and a large warm hand reached out and guided her down the hall passed her bed chamber. Lightening hot desire flew to her chest and stomach. She knew where they were going. She should protest, should dig her heels into the carpet and demand to be let go. Should not want what may happen behind his bed chamber door, but Lord help her she did. Wanted whatever he was willing to give. It would help on the cold nights alone int the future. She could bury herself under the covers and dream about this. About him.

∼

"We have to talk," Bastion whispered as he took the last few strides to his bedchamber door double checking that the hallway was clear on both ends before opening the door, guiding her in. He had been itching for her touch since she left his bed after they made love the first time.

"Stay." He demanded as the door shut behind him Bastion went to the adjoining room to see if his nephew was in residence. The room was empty and a note on the table said they had gone with a footman to the pond to practice fishing and examine the wildlife. The plan was to be back in time for dinner. It would be several hours before their return.

When he walked back into the room Aisling was where he left her, with the most enticing expression. It was a mix of anger and desire. She wanted to be angry with him, but her own desire and remembered emotions were making it a battle. They would end up in bed, but he would allow her the anger for the time being, because he too was angry at Aisling putting herself in danger.

"What were you thinking putting yourself in danger earlier?" Not bothering to care he shed his coat and cravat. "I told you. I was getting some air. I despise being cooped up." She answered, jutting out a stubborn chin and squaring her shoulders. "Besides, I was safer walking around my own home in the light of day than you were traveling Lord knows where in the dark of night on roads you are not familiar with."

"This is not about me. I can handle myself, but you may not be able to fend off an attacker like the one in the rose garden," She took in a large breath to speak and he put up a finger in protest before she could breathe a word. "And before you say you will just yell and scream again, I feel pressed to tell you not all men are averse to a woman's screams or cries, and by the time someone comes to your rescue the bastard will have already done what he had planned."

Bastion was satisfied that settled in the correct recesses of her very busy mind when she opened her mouth to protest, blinked, closed it, blinked again and stood silent. "I am more than willing to share with you where I was and what I was doing last night, but I cannot bare to think that you will be as foolish another time to take such leave with your own safety. I cannot be in Spain worrying about you."

Sadness skittered across her face, but she masked it quick enough. He never wanted to see sadness settle in the corner of her eyes again but wasn't sure how to make that happen. Bastion pulled his shirt over his head and tossed it on the chair to his writing desk. His task was almost complete, but they had now. He sauntered to the only woman who could drive him mad but didn't reach for her. She needed to come to him. To show him she wanted this again. His need was evident for any fool to see, but a woman's body was more circumspect and guarded.

She reached out and put a tiny, delicate hand on his cheek. Years of anger and near madness melted away at the touch. He couldn't wait any longer. He reached around her and pulled her to him burying his face in her neck and just stood there. This woman was a balm, a grounding point. She brought him to this place and is the connection from his present and his past. If his visions were to be believed his future. Thanks to her his nephew would know where his heritage, and Bastion would know his own story. Thanks to her the title his brother handed down to him fit now. He belonged to something other than himself and it was this small and mighty woman who did it. Did it all.

"Bastion?" she whispered the question into the top of his

head pressing kisses there. Need welled to overflowing. Without a word he scooped Aisling up against him and strode to the bed, setting her bottom down leaning in sending them both backward, he splayed below him. Placing his forearms on either side of her head to hold his weight, careful to slide his arms under the thick mass of hair which was strewn from its pins. God she was beautiful.

"Beleza."

"What?" she asked looking up at him.

"Beauty. Love you are a true beauty." He kissed the top of her nose. Setting his focus on ridding her of all her clothes starting with the blue ribbon that had taunted him in the drive earlier. One tug and it was nothing but strands of ribbon trailing down the sides. He pulled enough to free the buttons holding the back and top of the dress together. Once the buttons were undone he yanked her shoulders free and lower to expose beautiful breasts. She wiggled free from the sleeves. Her breasts were not large and buxom. They were small mounds that would be covered by one of his hands. They also would fit perfectly in his mouth. He always considered a woman with large breasts preferable, but not anymore. She was perfect.

Moving to stand at the edge of the bed to rid her of the flimsy slippers kissing the tips of her stockinged toes and setting each foot on each of his shoulders. The blush she produced must have gone to the top of her head and it made him smile.

His.

She belonged to him. No matter where he was in the world that fact would remain true, He kissed the calf of one leg then the other and worked his way up to delicate knees before giving her his best rakish smile while licking the underside of her still stockinged right knee. He reveled in how responsive his lady's body was. She was still very much an innocent. She knew now the panicle they would strive for but was still unaware of the pleasures there were to have beforehand, Aisling instinctively knew and responded to his touch. He watched as surprise and shock played on her pink face but continued licking his way down to one inner thigh until his tongue slid onto bare skin above the ribbon tied there. Bastion moved to the left knee and bestowed the same attention, but this time, he flipped the skirts over her waist to bare her and knelt at the edge of the bed, draping both legs over his shoulders so her knees rested there, hung down his back. Without a word, because there were no words in his vast vocabulary that could punctuate this perfect moment, he bent his head and tasted. His arm draped over her hips and abdomen to keep them on the bed. A sharp intake of breath and deep moan made him harden more, making him moan into her body. She tasted of honey, and musk, and something a little spicy that was only Aisling. If he never experienced love making again, this memory would carry him till death.

Her panting quickened and motions more frantic until her hands found his hair. She drove both hands into his hair holding his head in place. He smiled and laved faster and harder. When the passion wracked her body, she went limp. While she laid coming back to earth he rose and lifted a passion quenched Aisling enough to slide the dress over her hips and let it fall in a wrinkled bunch on the carpet Letting the stockings follow. When they joined he wanted no barriers.

"Aisling?" leaning in he bent close to her ear, giving it a nibble.

"Mmm."

"How are you my sweet? Are you ready for more?"

"Mmm, I think I may expire if you do anymore to me." She

answered in a lazy, thoroughly tumbled voice with a husky tone that sent his nerves all firing at once.

"Oh, but what a way to go." He answered and swung her farther up on the bed so that she lay in a pile of pillows no longer dangling from the edge. Wasting no time, Bastion dropped his breeches, climbed over her, and just watched as the haze of pleasure lifted slightly, with a smile that spoke of many nights of passion.

"Touch me Aisling." Bastion whispered not able to draw his eyes from hers. She reached out and with the lightest touch ran her fingers down his chest to his belly button. The other hand followed. She sent ripples of sensation through his torso as her hands meandered up his sides and back down until she slid one hand below his hip and traced the cord like muscle from his hip to his cock. "Oh God, Aisling." Bastion ground out. Neither of them may survive this coupling.

He let her explore and become more comfortable with touching him, until he couldn't take it anymore. Reaching down, pulling her hand from his erection, he brought it to his lips and kissed the tips of each finger. "Are you ready?" not sure he could accept anything but at this point. She nodded, and Bastion bent his head and took her mouth in his. Aisling was his and he was going to brand her with his kiss, his touch, and his love making.

He slid in with no barrier this time. She was ready for him and Bastion drank in her sigh. They fit like one half of the other. moving slowly, she wound her arms around his shoulders and pulled herself closer to him. Bastion took the hint and leaned in more fully pinning her to the bed. They moved as one, like they had been making love together forever. All too soon Aisling's body tightened, and a strangled sound caught deep in her throat.

The need to watch Aisling's orgasm play out on her face filled him. That amazing unguarded face. The stark pleasure shown like a sunbeam and it drove straight into his heart. He vowed in that moment that no other man would ever have the opportunity to see Aisling in the height of pleasure. She was his and he would go where she bade for the rest of his existence.

Not able to hold off Bastion tumbled into pleasure with her. Love making had never been so powerful for him, no woman did to him what she could. He collapsed next to her and flipped the blanket over to cover their sweat glistened bodies and waited for the passion to lift.

After several minutes of silence in the room Aisling spoke, "Where were you last night? You said you would tell me." She was rubbing his side from his buttocks to his arm pit. He doubted she realized, but he didn't say anything her touch was like a balm. He recounted his talk with the priest and what he learned of his ancestors and Aisling didn't judge, she just kept touching him.

"I remember a story about that. I never thought it was true."

"Yes, all three siblings. Apparently, the husband of one and the wife of the brother were able to steal the children from the horror and raised them as their own."

"And you had no idea?" Aisling asked rolling up on her side to face him.

"My mother always said she would tell us the story of our ancestors, but she died of a fever before she had a chance, and there were no records that I could find. My family history stops in France, with no idea of where any other relatives might be. The priest is sending over a load of journals and any research that had been done over the years to try and find relatives."

"And what is it you are doing this evening that I am not to be involved in?" Aisling asked giving him a pointed look. Bastion noted that in the future if he didn't want to have these types of discussions he needed to leave the bed, before the haze of pleasure left her eyes.

"I had a vision."

"I assumed." She answered saying no more. Bastion sighed and continued metering his words to give enough to satisfy her, but not enough to get her into trouble. He had rolled onto his back Aisling's head nestled in the crook of his arm, he began toying with a lock of chestnut hair that had splayed across his chest.

"When I met the woman, she was kind, but she held back. I took her hand. To anyone watching it appeared a gesture of support, but as soon as we made contact I could see it. See what she could not tell me. It all spilled out. It was the maid. Once the pregnancy was realized the servant girl wished revenge."

"What else did you see?" She asked too perceptive for her own good.

"I saw the bastard who threatened her to lie. I saw how scared the elderly woman was of him, and I saw how he is controlling her. I will end that tonight and the rest of this charade his is trying to orchestrate and I will find out why he is doing this to your family. I promise." Aisling stiffened in his arms. She should be happy it was almost over.

"When will you and Niall leave for Spain?" She asked. The question hit him in the gut.

"I am not sure. Our tickets are for any ship from the company at any time as long as they have a berth available, so we would have to send a rider to see when the next one was."

"Oh, I have never traveled out of England. I wasn't sure how that worked." She answered. He kissed the top of her head, because he did not want to see the pain filling those eyes again. He just pulled her closer to him and held on as the afternoon sun moved slowly across the room. Once it was time, he helped Aisling dress and watched as she pinned the riot of hair enough to get her to her room without undue attention. Aisling had been quiet since asking about his leaving and he didn't pry, consumed by his own thoughts just having the comfort of another person, this person, next to him was a comfort.

Just as she righted herself and shoved the forgotten stockings into a pocket the door of the adjoining room burst open and Niall and all his energy flooded the room. Bastion thanked the gods or his ancestors, or dumb luck for the timing. They had both dressed enough and the one who looked quizzical was Niall's tutor who had the good sense to nod his head and turn back into his part of the room

"Uncle, Uncle! You should see the fish we caught!" The little boy said in Spanish.'

"English, Niall. It is rude not to include everyone in a room in your conversation." Bastion said patting the boy on the head affectionately.

Niall turned to Aisling and bowed, even though it was not necessary, "Miss Lightowler, I caught a fish. A big one!" He said barely able to stand still with his excitement.

"Oh, Niall, that is wonderful. Did you give it to cook to prepare for your dinner?" She asked, leaning down to his height.

The boy nodded, "Yes we did and cook said it was bigger than the fish His Lordship catches."

"Oh, I am sure it was." Aisling agreed. Her face showed Bastion how much affection she had for his nephew and wished Niall had the love of a mother in his life. Aisling would be a fabulous mother for any child... He had already seen it.

CHAPTER 18

*A*isling had remained in Bastion's room until he was dressed to leave. He assured her with a kiss that it would be over soon. The cold that seeped into her bones had not left. She sat at dinner with no appetite but forced herself to eat as to not rise suspicion. Deidra would hold the secret close, but Maria and Constance need not know. Soon enough this would be over, and they would be free to marry and move out.

She had already decided not to marry if she had to care for their father and her sisters knew that, so it was easier to just allow them to think that.

Aisling was certain Bastion was putting himself in grave danger for her family. He stood nothing to gain by confronting the evil man who perpetuated all this. What would she do if some harm came to him? She could not live with herself. Thinking of the story of Corinthia and Lord Landry, how his body was found in what would have been the stairway to where his fiancé perished. Could he have saved himself? Did William remain because she was gone, and he could not live without her? Aisling understood that now.

She could go and try to pry his destination from Pilchard but knew it would not gain her any information. Pilchard was loyal and even a hint of the family being in danger would send his protective sensibilities into action. She would just have to wait.

"I hope Senor Guaire doesn't take long," Maria was complaining. "I want to go to bed with this curse lifted. I think I am getting wrinkles from tossing and turning."

"You don't get wrinkles from tossing and turning, and we will all have wrinkles eventually." Constance chided. "It is what adds character to the face." She put in as the artist she was.

"Hmm." Maria pouted.

"There really is no reason for any of us to stay up later than usual," Deidra reasoned. "He will be here when it is done, and I rather think it is not something that is going to be expedited to help with your sleeping."

"Aisling, will you be going to Spain Senor Guaire and his nephew leave? I do hope you marry here first so that we can all attend." Maria asked, sending Aisling into a panic.

She took a deep breath before saying, "Whatever are you talking about? I am not getting married, much less moving to Spain. The count and I have no interest in each other."

Maria's expression was one of shock and annoyance.

"Now, that expression may just give you wrinkles," Deidra chimed in. Aisling appreciated her sister trying to change tact, but Maria was tenacious.

"We have all seen the two of you. I can say I never thought a love match could progress in the matter of a week or so, but the two of you should be commended for your speed. Perhaps you do not realize it yet, but the two of you are in love." Maria continued as she paced to the window to look out into the darkness. "I think he is very nice and I approve. He is bigger than an actual Viking and I do not see the appeal. I will prefer a man much closer to my own size. Just having the count in the room seems to take the air out of it, but you obviously have no aversion to his size." Maria added, and Aisling could feel her cheeks burning from remembering just that afternoon, being covered by his size and she would have to admit, that no, she was not averse to it one bit.

"I am certain we all knew before either of you." Constance put in.

"What? You don't notice anything that is going around you. Ever." Aisling said to her sister in shock.

"Well, I would think that would tell you how blatantly obvious the two of you were." Constance added with a bit of sarcasm.

Aisling stood in the room, looking at all her sisters who had been there for every milestone like sisters were wont to do. And she guessed that pain this raw would not be easy to hide soon.

"I appreciate your enthusiasm for my happiness, but he will not be staying after this mess is cleared up. He has already said they would be leaving on the first available ship, and there has been no discussion for my hand or for me to travel with him." She managed to get it out without her voice cracking, but the tears spilling unavoidable.

They all gathered around for comfort.

"That makes no sense," Maria shot out. "Tis obvious the big fool loves you. Why hasn't he asked for your hand yet?"

Deidra was nodding in agreement and Constance was as well. "I cannot imagine a Count would not do the noble thing and ask for your hand." Deidra said and covered her mouth as soon as she realized.

It only took Maria a second to pick up on the words, "Noble? Why does he have to be noble?" Her youngest sister looked from Deidra to Aisling and back, eyes wide. She sucked in a breath. "Oh, heavens. You did? You actually did?"

"I do not care to discuss it." Aisling said and tried to leave the circle, which now was not as comforting.

"What if you are with child?" Constance pointed out.

"Oh God," Aisling said feeling the color drain from her face. She sat slowly in a chair. "I hadn't even considered– I mean we never discussed–I–I." The thought of bearing Bastion's children thrilled her, but what sent fear racing through behind the thrill was if he didn't want the same thing. She would raise their child. She would just remain out of sight of society until her sisters were settled and married, then the scandal it would cause would not affect them. That is all.

"Alright, I think that will be about enough of that. We need to focus on one problem at a time. If in fact you are with child there is nothing we can do about it now, so let us get through this first scandal." Deidra said as she hurried Maria and Constance from the room. When she returned Aisling had not been able to move. Fear had its grip on her tight and true.

"What will I do?" Aisling asked Deidra. "I love him. I know that I love him, but he is leaving."

"You are a Lightowler woman. You will stand tall and do what must be done, but I have a feeling you won't have to do anything. Guaire does not show his cards easily, but I agree with Maria and Constance he loves you but may not realize it yet or be scared of it."

Aisling appreciated the support and their comforting words. She wanted to think Bastion was as equally affected but considered his words when they made love. He had called her love and said she was beautiful, but had not said he loved her, and had not included her in the discussion about leaving. At any rate the blasted man had to come back alive before they could discuss anything, so instead of dwelling on an unknown future, she decided to concentrate on wishing him home safe. That would have to get her through this night. She could force the issue of their relationship after. Sitting back and picking up the book of poetry now held little allure, but it would pass the time.

Bastion had scheduled to meet Lord Landry and Mr. Standthrope at the burned manor site requesting each man to meet him without letting the other know. Lord Landry would be first, because Bastion had a feeling he would want the facts before Standthrope arrived.

"Lord Landry, thank you for meeting me." Bastion greeted as the man arrived on horseback, with his beast of a dog trotting along beside. Bastion decided the dog was certain he too was a horse, just a smaller version. The dog padded up and sniffed his breeches, turned, and leaned into him, making Bastion take a step back. Reaching down Bastion patted the animal.

"Bennett likes you. I dare say that is a better endorsement than that of the king." Landry drawled as he dismounted and ambled over. "He actually likes very few of my acquaintances."

"Well, I am thankful of his adoration. I am certain I would not like the opposite."

"No, you would not. So, why am I out here at dark Guaire?" Landry asked.

"I have found proof of what happened eighty years ago and who has brought this new version to light." Bastion waited to see if any sign of Landry being privy to the plot shown on his face, but nothing but pure curiosity shone back.

"Do tell. I would love for this mess to be cleared up. I do not even care what the outcome is. If we are wrong, the Lightowlers are put back into society as the paragons they were, and we are out nothing in truth. If the Lightowlers are proven to have a murderer in their ranks my father gains his land." Landy finished, but Bastion needed to point out the obvious.

"And the Lightowler women are thrust from society deemed unfit to wed and are ruined for the rest of their lives."

"Yes, you are right there. That would be damnable. I have no issue with the girls. I told you before I think them all good ducks. We were childhood playmates. I would hate to see them come to a bad end." Desmond assured Bastion. "What is it you have?" Bastion led Landry over to a wall that was still half standing, and he had laid out all the tangible proof he had. The journal entries, the note tucked inside of the backing on the back cover, the most damnable of all, the box, note, and fake ring from Aisling's mis adventure, and waited.

Bastion told him of the box and its contents first and Landry gaped in horror that Aisling was almost beaten with a shovel when she found him before he was finished. Bastion went through the other pieces pulling the old rotted bag from his satchel he found at the very site they were at. "I found this buried over here where the front hallway would have stood." He held it over the lamp so that Landry could see the metal tag of his family name still affixed to the outside. "If you smell it, because it was canvas, the smell of the gun powder and the oil are still very strong.

Landry put it up to his nose and turned away quickly, "Lawd, I see what you mean."

"I am going to assume that even eighty years ago the young

Lord Landry would not have carried such a bag with him?" Bastion asked, but already knew the answer.

"No. No, this is a bag that the servants use for moving goods. We have many of them in the stables, so that when we travel with the horses, we can keep our smaller tack clearly marked as ours."

The most important piece of evidence I have here is this note that I found in this journal. It was stuck under the back paper that covered the inside back cover. Landry read the note and blanched.

"I also have a witness to what happened. She was a child in your family's employ during that time. Unfortunately, she is being threatened to tell a different version of events, but once I take that threat away I am certain she will have a very different version of events to tell."

Hooves thundered up the trail. Standthrope swung into the clearing dressed like this was not to be his only stop this evening.

"Ho there!" he waved and dismounted leaving his horse to graze. "I say, good evening gentlemen. What antics are we to get up to?" Standthrope asked.

"Standthrope, what do you know of this?" Landry asked waving to all the evidence.

"I have no idea. I just got here. What is it?" He asked with no guile apparent.

"This," Bastion picked up the journal and the letter, that he would not be letting out of his grasp for the duration, "is a journal and note from your great-great grandmother confessing to the murder of her lover and his fiancé."

Standthrope to his credit gave a good impression of shock, but it didn't go fully into his eyes. "I have no idea–"

"Oh, please," Landry cut in. "This makes total sense. My

father knew, didn't he? He knew what really happened and brought you in to help with the charade. Why? Was it because Deidra turned you away?"

This was news to Bastion and once he heard that it all clicked into place.

Standthrope, didn't bother to try and deny it any longer. Apparently, when Deidra cuts a man she does it with aplomb.

"That bitch would be lucky to have me! I may not have a title, but I should have. It was her family that cheated my family out of it. I would be a Landry today, if not for her family." He spat. "I was the one who went to your father after hearing him lament wanting this piece of land. It took very little convincing on my part and he was a key player."

Bastion was not sure of the relationship between and young and senior Landry, but from the bland look on Landry's face he was not surprised and not about to come to his father's defense.

"Why after all these years?" Bastion asked "You are a good looking fellow, with passable manners. Couldn't you find another girl in the district?"

"I could have, but the Lightowlers have no sons. If I could wretch a son from Deidra I would have been set."

Landry helped to clarify, "Standthrope here is a bit of a gambler, and not a very good one. He is in need to marrying money or he will be ruined himself. What did my father offer to pay you, if you could pull this off?" Landry asked through gritted teeth.

"Ten Thousand" Standthrope admitted.

"Holy hell, my father has gone mad!" Landry spit out in shock.

Bastion had heard enough, he stepped forward to take a hold of Standthrope, but before he could Standthrope produced an angry looking pistol.

"That will be far enough." Andrew said waving the weapon at them both.

"I can't believe that those women would have the gall to try and best me." clearly stuck on the fact the Lightowlers were going to be his family's demise again. Bastion quite thought that perhaps it was bad breeding that had great-great grandmother and great-great grandson failing from the same ailment, revenge.

"You were the one in the rose garden?" Bastion asked as he tried to keep him talking and distracted.

"What self-respecting woman wanders the grounds at such an early hour. I had thought to go overnight, but was too tired after an evening out, so I decided it would safe to sneak over just at dawn. The chit had the nerve to come toward me? What woman does that? Comes at a man?"

Bastion smirked knowing that if she had thought to beat him with the shovel first she probably would have. As they kept Standthrope talking Bastion watched the shadows behind him cut the distance until two burly men grabbed him from behind. Before they wrestled the gun from him it fired into the night and Bastion heard Landry to his left swear and hit the ground.

"Landry?" Bastion yelled.

"I'll live. Doesn't feel like it went through. Grazed my arm. He always was a lousy shot."

The two men, who had been sent by the magistrate had Standthrope well under control.

"What shall we do with him?" Landry asked coming next to Bastion who was standing over the villain of the very bad play wanting in the worst way to rip him limb from limb for putting Aisling and her family in danger, not to mention talking so badly about Deidra, who had impeccable taste as far as Bastion could tell.

"I am not sure." Bastion answered. They could send him to the magistrate and prosecute, but who's to say how long he would be incarcerated and if his taste for revenge was so strong, he might well come back another time.

"I for one would love to see him cast out from the district for good. Nothing good could come of him ever coming back here." Landry mused.

"I think I may be able to orchestrate that," Bastion said reaching into his pocket and pulling out the papers showing full payment safe passage for three to Spain. Bastion certainly did not want Andrew Standthrope in his home country either, so he instructed the men to take him post haste, without stopping to the docks of London and speak with the shipping office about using those three tickets for one very long voyage one way to parts unknown. The men thought that a wonderful idea, but before Bastion let them depart, he went up to Standthrope, got very close and whispered, "If I hear of you being back in England, even stepping foot on English soil, or coming within one hundred miles of any of the Lightowler family, I will decimate you. I will rip you into so many small pieces Landry's dog won't even want to bother with you. The Lightowlers are now and forever under my protection. I assure you I have many talents at my disposal to get this job accomplished if I need to."

He was satisfied when Standthrope leaned heavily on one of his guards and his face was as white as his hair in the candle light. They would never see Standthrope again, of that he was sure.

"My dog never liked him. Perhaps I need to pay more credence to his opinion. He doesn't like my father either." Landry quipped as they watched the men haul Standthrope into a carriage and rumble away.

"What will you do with your father?" Bastion asked.

"I am not sure yet. I guess I will have to confront him and see where we go from there, but I assure you that the Lightowlers have nothing further to fear from our family. I personally promise that. And thank you for coming to their aide."

"Thank you, I will pass that along to the family, and as far as coming to their aid, Miss Aisling is not one to take no for an answer." Bastion said warily.

"That she is not." Landry laughed. "I will expect an invitation to the wedding breakfast." slapping Bastion on the back before ambling over to mount his horse, he took the reins of Stand-thrope's abandoned mount and left.

Bastion stood in the candle light and was not sure what had just happened, but he believed Desmond was now a friend for life and Bastion may have admitted he was about to ride back to the Lightowlers and propose to Aisling.

CHAPTER 19

*A*isling had put the poetry book down three times but kept picking it back up to try and force herself to concentrate on something, anything other than what could be taking him so long. Deidra settled sofa, and Maria and Constance were in attendance as well. To her surprise so was Papa. Lord Lightowler was ensconced in a chair next to the fire reading, but he was there.

"Senor Guaire has arrived!" Pilchard bellowed from the front hall and before Aisling could rise, Bastion strode into the parlor.

"It is done. Your family will be publicly cleared of any misdoings from eighty years ago. Landry promised to see to it."

"Who was it?" Aisling asked, still not able to stand, legs weak from relief that he was safe. She didn't want to see him leave, but this horrible thing was over, perhaps Mama would return, and life would go back to normal, she thought for everyone, save her.

"Standthrope." Bastion announced the name and Deidra

sank back onto the sofa where she had been sitting between Maria and Constance.

"Mr. Standthrope?" Deidra asked. Maria had sat and was patting Deidra on the shoulder for comfort.

"I am afraid so. You scorned him, and his fragile ego could not handle that, not to mention he had to marry because he was broke."

"I know," Deidra said through tears. "That is why I rejected him. I told him I could not marry a man who had no more desire to be stable than a foolish squirrel who squanders his money." She burst into tears. "I did this, this is all my fault!" she cried into shaking hands.

Bastion walked over to Deidra, who was quickly becoming the sister he never had and took her by the shoulders lifting her to standing. Squeezing her shoulders so she looked up at him. "This had nothing to do with you. Nothing. Do you understand me? This was about a man who wasn't a man at all. He harbored a grudge with your family for taking his title away from him, when years ago Lord Landry chose to parish with his fiancé instead of marrying the maid he got with child. This had nothing to do with you."

Deidra nodded, and Bastion pulled her into a quick hug.

"What of the Landry's involvement?" Mr. Lightowler asked.

"Desmond Landry was totally unaware of the agreement Standthrope had made with his father. He was present this evening and after Desmond gets his arm tended I have an idea he and his father will be having a very uncomfortable and heated conversation, but Landry has asked me to assure you that the Lightowlers will see no more conflict from the Landry's and he hopes that your friendship can remain."

"What happened to his arm?" Constance asked.

"Standthrope shot him. Just a flesh wound. He will be fine."

Aisling was glad she still was not standing, at the mention of a gun being involved the dinner she had not wanted threatened to make another appearance.

Bastion treaded to Aisling and knelt down. He smelled like night and beeswax, and horses. She reveled in it.

"You have not had much to say." Bastion said settling his hands on hers that were fisted together in her lap.

"There is nothing more to add. You have done what I asked of you, and I will be forever grateful for saving my sisters' reputations. I am very glad you are not injured." She added but could not bear to look him in the eye.

Bastion reached up and tipped her chin toward him. "There is much more to say and discuss, and I am certain I will never have a quiet moment for the rest of my life, but I have to ask. Miss Aisling Lightowler, will you do me the great honor of becoming my wife?"

The silence stretched and settled in the room, not even a breath could be heard.

"I– I don't understand."

"I didn't either until I was holding you. I loved you from the first letter you sent me. You were pulling me from a life that was dead. I had no past, my present was nothing but trying to relive a past with my brother and mother, and I could not see beyond my own grief to see a future. But what I saw was you. You are my future. You are a bridge. My destiny."

Aisling could not speak, tears streaming down her face she nodded. Taking his hands that still rested in her lap drawing them up to kiss them.

Her sisters erupted in cheers, and Papa yelled for Pilchard to get some of the good wine and glasses for all including the servants, but it all faded to a din as Bastion pulled her from the chair and wrapped her in an embrace.

"What of your visions?" Aisling whispered in his ear.

"Visions of you Aisling, only visions of Pleasure for me now." He said and kissed her. The spell was broken when her sisters muscled their way between the couple to share their happiness, but Aisling didn't mind, very soon she would wake in those arms every morning and be lulled to sleep in them every night. It didn't matter if they were in England or Spain, she just wanted to be with him and to be part of his past, his present, and his future.

<<>>

Ruination of a Rogue

Prologue

December, 1814

"Love's first blush that paces the heart like the most delicate petal from the youngest bud, bring together that which was once one, but have wandered apart searching for the light of the candle blessed by the drawing power of the full moon and sealed with the blood of the soul searching to be united again and made whole."

Aisling looked at the fragile worn piece of paper, the incantation starting to fade with age and being folded so many times and placed inside the locket.

"Most wives would hope the first piece of jewelry they are handed by their husband would be for them."

"Yes, I suppose they would. However, I would like to believe that my own power brought us together across two countries. I am hopeful that I am the lost half of your soul so you will have no further use of such an amulet." Bastion's smooth Spanish accent colored even the most mundane terms and Aisling was still trying to not be as affected when he spoke.

"You said this belonged to your mother?" Bastion had been back in England for a month now. He had not bothered to show her the antique pendent until now. Why he had waited was a question.

"Yes, the family story goes something akin to, my mother wanted to find her soulmate before she was set to wed the second Count of Lugar de Sueno, arranged by her father. Her father gave her one full moon cycle to find that one man she could not be without. My mother, using all that her mother had taught her, handed down from many generations of witchcraft, got to work creating a spell, that if practiced on the full moon would help find the one true love."

"And did it work?" Enthralled with Bastion's storytelling, Aisling still struggled to grasp that she was now wed to not only a Spanish count, but also one with a long lineage of witches, of which he was one.

"According to my mother, it did. Her love ended up being the local count her father chose. She thought she didn't want to marry him, but they were happily married in a love match for the rest of her life."

Aisling cocked an eyebrow, "Then perhaps the spell never worked, and your mother just married the man her father wanted her to."

"Perhaps that is the case," Bastion admitted. "However, my mother was not the type to lean toward convention or to be told what to do, even by her father."

He picked up the pendent and his large hand swallowed the delicate necklace. Aisling watched him turn it over and shift it to catch the light. It was beautiful, the green opal in the center sparkling with its darker and lighter veins flowing throughout the gem. The setting was of brass, but as delicate as the chain that it would hang from. It was round and had a lacy design that made one think of the moon when they looked at it. Any woman would be happy to wear such an item.

"What do you intend to do with it? If you brought it all the way from Spain, you must have a use for it."

Bastion, set the necklace down and drew her into his embrace. His warmth surrounded Aisling like a blanket, a blanket she missed every night until his return. And that made her remember he would once again be leaving, returning to

Spain. After this trip, they would remain in London. She would be away from her family, but she would be with her husband. She looked up into his eyes, which saw more than anyone she had ever known.

"As a matter of fact, I do. I know you are anxious to see your sisters settled, and it would go a long way to allowing some comfort once I am back and we are in London, if you knew your sisters were also set into their own households."

"You are not wrong. I fear that if left to their own, none of them will marry for love and perhaps not at all, in Constance's case. She is too like Father and stays pre-occupied with her sculpting. If a man doesn't get dropped into her studio, she may never marry. And Diedra is so preoccupied with making sure our parents' home runs smoothly, she hardly has time or interest to be in search of a man to give her, her own home to run. But, as far as Maria is concerned, this trip to our Godmother's for her twelfth night ball and house party, may be her only chance to find a husband she finds suitable."

Aisling left the safe confines of her husband's arms and went back to packing what few items she had left for their trip. They would be leaving the next day. It was safer to travel in the north of England on nights when the moon was at its largest, so the timing was actually quite good.

"My plan for this amulet is to gift it to Maria, and tell her when she has no use for it any longer to pass it on to one of her sister's left to find their own soul mate."

Aisling turned, the surprise unable to be hidden from her expression. For the most part they had been able to keep Bastion's family history a secret from her family. Not at all that they were ashamed of it, but witches were still not accepted, and it was safer to keep her family in the dark about the truth in case they were ever questioned.

"How—"

Bastion put up a hand to stop her from worrying. "I intend for you and I to do the spell work. You are of the same blood-line as your sisters, so if I am correct in what little knowledge I have, your blood will be the same as using Maria's. Then when I give it to her, I will tell her the story of the amulet as if it is folklore. Only you and I will know the truth of it all."

She put the last of her writing tools in her traveling desk and closed the lid, then went back to the arms of her husband, who too soon would once again be traveling through the war to go back to Spain. "Do you really think it could help them all find their one true love?"

"That is my sinister plan." He squeezed her and growled low in her ear, sending a shiver of awareness through her. When they had their own townhouse in London, she was planning for them to not leave the bedchamber for a fortnight because they would not have worry about being disturbed by a house full of well-meaning people. But, before that, she had to get her youngest sister, Maria, safely through the house party and to the alter with no loss of reputation in between.

Bastion picked up the pendent and held the trinket box that protected a fresh rosebud petal from one of her father's rose bushes, a small unlit candle, and a tiny piece of white linen. "So, what say you? Want to dance in the full moon and cast spells like a proper witch?"

"As long as I do not have to do so naked. Tis too cold now in the year for that."

Bastion lifted her from the waist until her entire body nestled into his and waggled his eyebrows, "You think us heathens and not witches, my dear. We do the undressing in the warmth of the bedchamber, not out in the frigid night air."

He then nuzzled her neck and Aisling was lost. She knew if

he asked her to walk naked across the moor in January, she would do it. It warmed her to think her new husband felt such a kinship to her sisters that he would risk their finding out his family secret. Aisling, the ever-practical woman she was, sent a small prayer up to the heavens that the spell worked, because she felt that the lord would agree those three girls would need all the help from every sector of the universe to get them settled. It couldn't hurt.

ABOUT THE AUTHOR

Author of 7 Historical romances, including the Improper Wives for Proper Lords series, Clair Brett lives in NH with her ever emptying nest which includes her children when they visit, two cats, one willful dog boxer/beagle, and a mean Pitbull mix, that will lick you to death and run into her kennel when you speak loudly, and one grand dog who one day just moved in. And one ever harassed husband who takes it all in stride. A lover of all things Regency, Clair, was hooked when she first read Jane Austen. She is a firm believer that a reader finds a piece of who they are or learns something about the world with every book they read. She wants her readers to be empowered and to have a refreshed belief in the goodness of people and the power of love after reading her work.

Contact Clair

Website:
https://www.clairbrett.com
Facebook:
http://facebook.com/@AuthorClairBrett
Twitter:
http://twitter.com/@clairbrett
Goodreads:
https://www.goodreads.com/clairbrett
Pinterest:
https://www.pinterest.com/clairbrett
Patreon:
https://www.patreon.com/clairbrett
Bookbub:
https://www.bookbub.com/authors/clair-brett
Instagram:
https://www.instagram.com/clairbrettauthor/

Join Clair's Newsletter
https://www.clairbrett.com/newsletter-sign-up

ALSO AVAILABLE FROM CLAIR

Improper Wives for Proper Lords Series
Dealing with the Viscount
An Heiress by Midnight
Marked for Love
Courtesan's Wicked Desire

English Roses Series
Visions of Pleasure
Ruination of a Rogue

Stand Alone Novels
Winn's Fall

www.ingramcontent.com/pod-product-compliance
Lightning Source LLC
Chambersburg PA
CBHW020955180626
46814CB00003B/1100